JUN – – 2019

Still in Love

Still in Love

A Novel

MICHAEL DOWNING

COUNTERPOINT
Berkeley, California

Library of Congress Cataloging-in-Publication Data
Names: Downing, Michael, 1958– author.
Title: Still in love : a novel / Michael Downing.
Description: First hardcover edition. | Berkeley, California : Counterpoint, 2019.
Identifiers: LCCN 2018018897 | ISBN 9781640091474
Subjects: | GSAFD: Love stories.
Classification: LCC PS3554.O9346 S85 2019 | DDC 813/.54—dc23
LC record available at https://lccn.loc.gov/2018018897

Jacket design by Kelly Winton
Book design by Jordan Koluch

COUNTERPOINT
2560 Ninth Street, Suite 318
Berkeley, CA 94710
www.counterpointpress.com

Printed in the United States of America
Distributed by Publishers Group West

10 9 8 7 6 5 4 3 2 1

for Peter Bryant

Art is not what you see, but what you make others see.

EDGAR DEGAS

Still in Love

ONE

1.

By midmorning, a steady wind was sweeping the last of the snow showers north of Mark Sternum's house in Ipswich. He glanced out his kitchen window and nodded, grateful for the improving conditions. For most people in New England, this blustery Wednesday in January was just another winter day. But for Mark and the other adherents of the Hellman College academic calendar, it was the first day of the spring semester. He turned his gaze back to his computer screen and checked his word count for the zillionth time. He'd spent the last hour reading and rereading the short story he had written, lopping off words to pare it down to size. As far as he knew, the Professor had not concocted a revised version of the assignment, and Mark hoped his colleague wouldn't come up with any last-minute inspirations.

Although they'd co-taught the creative-writing workshop for ten years and were both tenured, Mark still deferred to the Professor in almost all substantive matters. Details were Mark's domain. He clicked through his Creative Writing files and printed thirty copies of the assignment for today's class, the first of the new semester.

TECHNICAL EXERCISE 1

The challenge is to write a story that fulfills the premise outlined in the scenario.

Scenario

There is a man in a room. There is a door, a window, and a chair in the room. Another man comes to the door. He says, "I'll be with you in a few minutes. Please don't open the window." He leaves. He returns. The window is open. Assume that readers know nothing. Your story begins as the second man returns and sees that the window is open, but readers will need to understand that he had previously told the man in the room not to open the window.

Technical Limits

1. No more than 250 words. (Along with your name, please put the word count on your story.)
2. Past tense.
3. Third-person narration. (The perspective can be limited or omniscient, and don't worry if you don't understand the distinction, which we will review and discuss later in class. The idea is simply to use the convention of a narrator who is not a character in the story.)

There was one additional Technical Limit in Mark's version of this assignment, but the Professor wasn't convinced it served the story, so, much as Mark loved it, he decided to drop it. For now. He could always change his mind and add it back in later.

Mark had written the original version of this and every assignment, as well as the syllabus, and he'd selected the readings, prepared the handouts, and scheduled the sequence of workshops. Mark alone would bother to learn the names of the students, ask them about their previous experiences as writers and their expectations for the course, squander a few minutes before class talking to them about the latest horror or hilarity that had streamed onto campus via YouTube, and spend hours every week with them in his office reviewing the finer points of syntax and grammar and discussing the tentative revisions they made to the first and second and eleventh draft of stories they were not eager to resubmit to the public workshop process until they were confident the new draft would be welcome news to the Professor. All of this—in fact, everything except the completed stories students wrote—was minutiae, trivia, inadmissible evidence in the court of the Professor. Mark didn't know if their division of labor was fair, or if the Professor's insistence on the strict separation of writing from writer was revolutionary or reactionary. But each of them seemed to think he'd got the better of the bargain.

It was the Professor who'd persuaded Mark to join the creative-writing program at Hellman when it was launched a decade ago. Enrollment in each workshop would be capped at twelve, and they'd be dividing the workload. Even so, the prospect was not initially appealing. Mark had spent almost twenty years at McClintock College in Boston not teaching creative writing. In fact, he'd voluntarily taught four sections of Basic Skills and Composition every semester just to avoid the inane task of reading original short stories written by students who reliably asked if the novels on the reading list were fiction or nonfiction. His one interview at Hellman was conducted by Althea Morgan, the diminutive chair of English, whose speech was inflected with a mild Jamaican lilt that made everything she said sound offhand, including her admission that she was counting on the new content-free writing courses to raise her department's sagging popularity.

Having written his doctoral dissertation on metaphoricity in Melville, Mark felt eminently qualified to teach nothing. But wasn't the job of teaching young people how to make something of nothing better left to the world's great religions?

Althea reminded him that he'd be required to teach only two courses per semester. And the Professor had promised to provide the ballast if Mark would simply design a course resembling a party boat that would attract hordes of unsuspecting students looking for a fun cruise around the shoals of the short story. Mark signed on.

The Hellman spring semester reliably opened on the third Wednesday of January. So, after the first meeting of the workshop today, Mark had nothing to do until Monday morning at 8:00 a.m., when he would happily spend a few hours collecting and collating the stories students wrote in response to their first assignment, make reading copies to be distributed at the second class meeting, and prepare an electronic version of the whole mess for the Professor, including the 250-word story he'd dutifully written to satisfy his belief that you shouldn't expect students to do something you couldn't do in the time allotted for any assignment. That was the limit of Mark's commitment.

For his part, the Professor would read and annotate each page of student prose with typed textual comments and questions keyed to marginal footnotes, and he would provide a separate narrative response, often twice as long as the story itself. This was better than what any published writer got from an editor or the *New York Times Book Review*. Mark could not imagine how he did it. But the Professor could not imagine why Mark bothered to write a new story for each Technical Exercise every semester, so according to the peculiar math of their relationship, they were even.

* * *

Technical Exercise 1.
(Mark Sternum / 250 words)

The door hinge creaked. Paul leaned in, grabbed his coat from the old club chair. "It's eight."

Mark groaned from the bed. "Come here."

"I'm late," Paul said.

"I said I'd make poached eggs."

"That was at six." Cold air streamed toward Paul like a tide.

Mark watched the tails of Paul's tweed coat fly by the bed.

Paul reached for the pane Mark had raised. "I told you to keep this closed."

"I told you not to take the gig in Rome."

Paul's hands drooped to the sill. "You said you'd take this spring term off."

"Did I?"

"Don't start." Paul turned to Mark. "Don't you teach soon?"

"Not till three."

"I should have stayed at my place." Paul pulled a Swiss knife from his coat, aimed the blade at the track.

Mark sat up. "I'll close that."

"It takes two—the track's bent." Paul huffed out a sigh. "I hate to rouse you, but my ride is here."

Mark joined Paul, saw the sleek black cab by the snow bank.

Paul said, "Grab the frame. On three, shut it. One, two—"

"Five months?"

"Three." Paul pulled the knife out, but Mark failed to slam down the pane.

The cab beeped twice.

They watched it drive off down the street.

"My bad," Mark said. "Spring break in Rome?"

"It's too late for this."

"I mean it."

Paul said, "So do I," and shoved Mark out, watched him fall to the ground. Mark just could not keep it closed.

* * *

2.

The morning's banked-up gray and purple clouds were spent, and the silvery, distant mid-January sun was doing its best to melt the remainder of the snow squalls from Mark's front steps and the windshield of his admirable and unreliable green Saab. Paul had texted from the security line at the airport and again when he reached his gate. They hadn't really spent their last morning together arguing about a window, but Mark really had overslept, and he had so often raised the possibility of taking a leave this semester that someone less patient with his dithering might have murdered him. And now, Mark wished he were in Rome, where Paul would be temporarily installed as the executive director of the first international outpost of the Paean Project, a research and training consortium of Boston teaching hospitals devoted to the study and management of public-health issues associated with homeless, migrant, and exiled populations.

There was a window in Mark's house that didn't shut properly, but it was not in the bedroom. It was in the kitchen, and Paul had pointed it out repeatedly, which was his idea of being handy. Mark had repeatedly feigned surprise, his way of protecting Paul from the knowledge that the entire house was constantly on the verge of collapse.

They'd lived together for thirty happy years, a feat they achieved by never quite living together. Paul kept a one-bedroom condo in a plain and sturdy brick building in Harvard Square and paid a monthly fee to keep things in operating order. Mark's tiny old house in Ipswich was a work in progress, and the most successful projects lately were the slow and steady crowning of the center beam that made the floor boards sink in the middle of every room, and the spread of a mysterious disease that was working like leprosy on the horsehair plaster walls, some of which had begun to resemble topographical maps veined with mighty rivers.

After he'd dressed and packed up his bag for school, Mark was still feeling bad about reneging on his poached-eggs promise, so he climbed up on the kitchen counter, boots in the sink, and shoved up the window. The track was bent, but it was made of ancient lead that could be pushed around like putty. The actual problem was a screw that he'd tightened once—once too often—which had bored a hole too big for itself in the wormy old wood and now stuck out, preventing the frame from dropping to the sill. With a couple of brass brads, Mark hammered the lead track back to where it belonged, and the offending loose screw obligingly popped out and landed somewhere in that dark continent between the wall and the kitchen counter. There was another window that didn't like to open or close in the tiny dining room

Mark had turned into his study, but he decided to save it for summer, so Paul could have the pleasure of misdiagnosing that problem.

3.

The Hellman campus was nineteen miles southwest of Mark's house in Ipswich and seventeen miles north of Paul's place in Cambridge. Hellman occupied one hundred handsome rural acres in the tony commuter village of Manning, Massachusetts, a former farming community wedged in between Wakefield and Saugus, one-time factory and tobacco towns. The college was founded in 1891 as the Hellman School of the Arts by the notable English plein–air painter Samuel Hellman. Hellman was well into his sixties when he landed in Boston in 1890, and the idea for his school was inspired by the efforts of his former colleagues in England, who were busy establishing the famous Newlyn School and art colony when Hellman took off—a sudden departure inspired by his socially dicey second marriage to the fantastically wealthy Esha Goswami, the sixteen-year-old daughter of an Indian diplomat.

Esha's fortune funded the purchase of one hundred acres in Manning when the town was selling off a vast parcel of land known as Breakheart Reservation. That reservation land had a rich and wild history that began more than ten thousand years ago, when the paleo-americans hunted and farmed there and, more recently, included a sizable seventeenth-century ironworks, eighteenth-century sawmills, nineteenth-century sailcloth manufacturers, and a recurring snuff-making operation. All of the commercial ventures eventually failed, and the acreage abutting the campus was reforested and turned over to the Metropolitan Parks System of Greater Boston.

Hellman's school survived, as did the controversial marriage of its founder. By 1895, Esha had organized a wide-ranging program of classes in language and domestic arts taught by enterprising young women who'd found their way to Boston from all over the world and were eager to land somewhere safe. In 1899, the thriving Hellman School of International Culture and Art hired the entire faculty of a nearby boarding school destroyed by fire and emerged in the twentieth century as Hellman College.

These days, its arts and language programs reliably ranked in the Top Ten in the country according to the influential annual lists published by failing magazines that could no longer afford to distribute printed copies of their publications. Sixteen hundred undergraduates shelled out more than $60,000 a year to live in twin-bedded rooms within walking distance of Breakheart Reservation's two man-made lakes and the fossilized and rusty remains of ten thousand years of failed agricultural and industrial enterprises.

And yet, higher education in America was allegedly in crisis.

This was difficult to discern if you drove, as Mark did, through the stately stands of Italian pines and leathery green rhododendrons braving swales of snow on the lower campus, past the midcentury brick theater, concert hall, three gymnasiums, and the cascading lines of dorms that resembled high-end motels with their French doors, iron balconies, and views to Breakheart Hill. A sharp left or right led to acres of free underground parking, and after a brief elevator ride, Mark emerged on the edge of the large Common, a collection of handsome five-story, white-brick classroom and administration buildings surrounding the preserved barn-board houses and meeting halls that constituted Hellman's original campus, and a knee-deep pond, presently occupied by three unstable ice-skaters holding hands.

Mark's office was on the second floor of Humanities Hall—Hum Hall to faculty, Hmmm Hall according to undergraduates. His was one of dozens of eight-by-twelve white rectangles with a window, a Scandinavian teak desk, chair, and bookshelves lining an entire wall, and a black Hellman alumni chair for student visitors, all standard-issue for full-time faculty. In the fall, Mark had agreed to share his office with a member of the adjunct faculty, most of whom were traditionally crowded into fifth-floor offices with four or five other part-timers. The redistribution of the non-tenured faculty was part of a pitiful stew of last-minute concessions cooked up by the administration when a national service-employees union began to circulate organizing materials to the adjuncts in the fall. However, Mark's new office mate didn't merit a second suite of Scandinavian teak. Instead, a white plywood desk and a plastic chair on casters from IKEA had been shoved under the window for the highly regarded translator and half-time Italian instructor Karen Cole.

Mark didn't mind sharing, especially this semester, as he was teaching only one workshop in the spring, having received a course release to act as Hellman's representative to the New England Private College Access, Justice, and Excellence (NEPCAJE) initiative. He did mind that his ancient, floppy, coffee-stained copies of the collected stories of Anton Chekov and Alice Munro had to share shelf space with the NEPCAJE reading list, whose contrarian titles sounded like teasers for upcoming exposés on competing cable-news channels: *Is College Worth It?*; *The End of College*; *The Future of College*; *The Rise of the All-Administrative University*; *Professors and the Demise of Education*; *Academically Adrift*; *College (Un)Bound*; *The Miseducation of the American Elite*; *Why Does College Cost so Much?*

Since September, Mark had commuted to seven of New England's premier private colleges and universities for NEPCAJE conferences and panel discussions. The sessions had yielded no solution to the alleged crisis in higher education, but the combined $75 billion in endowment funds at those nonprofit institutions was annually yielding about 12 percent. Right through November, Mark had played the part of a Hellman representative perfectly—arriving at events a few minutes late in jeans and one of Paul's venerable flannel shirts and proceeding to take copious notes, simply for the pleasure of watching his exemplary student behavior spread among his better-dressed Ivy League colleagues, inveterate grade-grubbers every one.

In December, however, Mark made two mistakes. During a roundtable discussion, when a dean from Amherst rhetorically asked how many of the assigned books anyone could be expected to read, Mark had answered "All of them. I did." And then the clutch on his Saab went, and instead of having it repaired, he commuted by train from Paul's apartment to campus for the last week of the semester, and he opted to skip a NEPCAJE meeting in Burlington rather than driving to Vermont in first gear. He was nominated in absentia to write the conference's literature review by that dean from Amherst, a draft of which was due at the end of March, one week after spring break.

Mark's phone pinged with a text. *a favor and a question—whats so bad about the forbes seminar room?*

Althea Morgan was retiring at the end of the spring semester, and having devoted the last decade of her career to chairing the English Department, she was calling in all of her chits. Since October, she'd also been calling in most days from the beachfront house in Jamaica she was renovating.

Mark wrote, *Stanhope or Elizabeth?* All of the classrooms and lecture halls in the old barn-board buildings were named for Newlyn School painters, and the only thing wrong with being assigned to teach in the Forbes room was that there were two, in two different buildings, named for the husband and wife painters. He added, *It snowed here this morning, in case you were feeling nostalgic.*

i wish. am on campus & feeling too f—ing cold to type. am standing in STANHOPE forbes rm & open window is too high to reach w/out risk to bum hip. can i switch your class to here and give your rm to annoying new adjunct teaching poetry?

Mark hesitated. The Professor had specifically requested a classroom in the Hum building so he wouldn't have to put on a hat and coat to commute across the Common to class.

Althea wrote, *correct answer is yes*

Mark relented, but he reminded her that his class met in about twenty minutes. *Can you have someone put up signs for students?*

they know—made switch this morning on StudentServe

Mark didn't respond. He did let the Professor know about the switch, and a few minutes after he'd logged in and out of StudentServe to confirm that Althea had anticipated his capitulation hours earlier, he received a revised version of the first assignment. As usual, the Professor had decided to change a couple of words and had utterly altered the assignment.

Scenario

There is a man in a room. There is a door, a window, and a chair in the room. Another man comes to the door. He says, "~~I'll~~ We'll be with you in a few minutes. ~~Please don't~~ Don't open the window." He leaves. He returns. The window is open.

Assume that readers know nothing. Your story begins as the second man returns and sees that the window is open, but readers will need to understand that he had previously told the man in the room not to open the window.

The Professor had nullified Mark's literary effort from this morning. Try as he might, Mark could not imagine Paul or any normal adult adopting the Royal We to address a spouse. The only other way to accommodate that "we" would be to add a second man alongside Paul at his bedroom door at eight o'clock in the morning, and that would be another story altogether. No, that change of pronoun and the deleted *Please* effectively shifted the scenario from the familiar to the formal, from the domestic to the professional.

Mark had just enough time to revise the assignment on his master file, print new copies for the students, and then run across the Common—and he'd already forgotten which Forbes room was his.

4.

It was exactly three o'clock when Mark rushed into the Elizabeth Stanhope Seminar Room, and there was exactly one student there to greet him, a thin young man with a shaved head sitting cross-legged on the floor, who scrambled to his feet and looked around apologetically. "I could try to find you a chair." His face was alarmingly red, either from the exertion of standing up or the absurdity of his surroundings. There was not a desk or chair in sight. There were dozens of primary-colored yoga mats arranged around a white canvas tepee. "I got here early so I could talk to you about leaving class early today. Is this Creative Writing?"

"Yes and no," Mark said, anticipating the delight of enduring the Professor's opening-day lecture about promptness. "Grab your coat and follow me. I'm Mark Sternum."

"I'm Anton." He tugged at the waistband of his yellow V-neck. "This is my coat."

"That's creative writing." Mark headed into the hall toward the exit, but Anton sped past him in time to hold open the front door. "Thank you. We're going left."

"I have an appointment. I tried to change it." Anton sped ahead and slid along a patch of ice that ran out as the walkway curved toward their destination. He was panting when he said, "I don't want you to think I'm that guy."

"Which guy?" Mark held open the front door of the Arts Building.

"It's with a doctor is all I mean. Wow." He pointed to the open door of the Stanhope Forbes Seminar Room. "Are they all in our class?"

"Not for long. After your appointment, email me and ask for today's assignment. I won't remember to send it along. I'm that guy." Mark waved Anton in ahead of him. "Now, try to look like we were talking about something literary."

Anton said, "Good luck finding a chair," and slid toward the back of the room.

Mark stood in the doorway for a few seconds as the buzz of conversation fizzled out. "My name is Mark Sternum, and as you may have heard by now, this is Creative Writing." He paused, but the Professor said nothing, something of a surprise. "If that doesn't tally with your expectations, please leave." He dropped his bag on one of the chairs at the head of the vast conference table, pulled out the stack of syllabi he'd printed, and slid it halfway down the table. "Everyone else, read through the syllabus, and in a few minutes, we'll try to figure out exactly who's here and what we think we're going to do this semester."

The room was charming—a ten-by-twenty box of pickled barn board, with six tall nine-over-nine paned windows set so deep into either side that the generous sills could be used as seats, which with the six black armchairs at either side of the table gave almost everyone a place to sit. Mark's initial count was twenty-six students, though the seating arrangements kept shifting, and at least two latecomers had drifted in. There were two black alumni chairs and plenty of space for him and the Professor at the front of the class, but the other end of the too-long table was shoved right up against the far wall, dead-ending anyone searching the back of the room for an unoccupied place to land.

Just before Mark made a stab at taking attendance, the Professor suggested it might make sense to have the twelve registered students take the seats at the table, but Mark thought that was more punitive than productive and simply called out the first names of the registered students, then the six on the wait list, two of whom were not present, and then he wrote down phonetic approximations of the names cheerfully called out by the additional thirteen hopefuls. "It's a bother, I know," he said as he finished his list, "but it matters, as the final enrollment will include only people here for the first class. So, well done for turning up today."

"But only twelve will be enrolled," said the Professor. He paused, and then using his voice like a gavel he said, "Twelve. Twelve. No matter how committed or eager or talented others may be, regardless of how long anyone else hangs around during the Drop-Add period, only twelve of you will be extended the extraordinary privilege of having a ready audience of intellectuals to read and respond to your original work. And just in case I haven't yet entirely extinguished the spirit of enthusiasm in the room, I'll review the requirements. After that, if you find your expectations defeated and your creative temperament offended, you should probably stick around. The rest should leave. In short, the rules are these: Be present. Be productive. In practice, here's how that happens."

The Professor opened with a word about phones and other electronic devices—"No."—followed by no extensions, no excuses, no letter grades on work in progress, and "I will have no interest whatsoever in why you were not in class, where you were, or who else was involved in your absence. Will I ever consider anything more important than our time together? No." Mark had heard this speech dozens of times, and he'd also translated it into more positive terms for the syllabus. He knew what was coming. During their first few years together, he'd often interrupted the naysaying with explanations—*You can always come to my office to ask about your standing in the course, but the goal is not to have grades be the principal currency between us in the classroom.*—and interpretations—*Of course, you are adults with complicated lives, so you'll simply email me in the event of an emergency involving you or a loved one.* But instead of reassuring students, Mark's comments unnerved them and provoked endless questions and speculation. *Stepparent, housemate, dog, tennis partner—which qualified as a loved one? If I email my story before 8:00 a.m. on Monday, but the Hellman system bounces it back to me for some reason and I have to resend it, will it count? You said we don't have to include every story in our final portfolio, and we do have to revise every story we do include, but you didn't say how many times we should revise the stories we are including and whether including only one or two will lower our grade when we finally get it, when it will be too late to do anything about it.*

So Mark had learned to smile through the negativity and not miss his cues. The few students who were genuinely upset by what they heard would come to Mark's office before the next class to confess their fears and anxieties. If they ever wanted to talk to the Professor, Mark never heard about it. They were peers in rank, and age, and pretty evenly matched physically, too, but it seemed to Mark that time had been a little greedier with the Professor. He still had his hair, but it was lighter brown, silvered at the edges and almost translucent in bright light. His body sometimes seemed more frame than flesh lately, especially when he took off his jacket and his uniform Levi jeans swagged like a hammock from his hip bones. And every year, students seemed to find it harder to tell if the Professor was amused or annoyed as his gaze narrowed and his face became an aggrieved etching of itself, but maybe that was just as true of Mark, just as true of everyone over fifty, when so many amusements seem more intrusive than inviting, more annoying than alluring.

When would the Professor want to discuss ideas for stories? Never. When would it be useful to disclose the autobiographical basis of a story? Never. How much time will we spend brainstorming and writing in class? None. "I will never be interested in anything except every word you write," the Professor said, pausing for the first time in a while. "And no one will ever be more engaged by your choices, more alert to your intentions, more mindful of the gap between your reach and your grasp, more fascinated by every word on the page, the syntax of every sentence, the intentional allusions and the many fortuitous suggestions present in your text. Oh, and what did he say about extensions?"

Mark said, "He doesn't believe in them."

"What did he say was the only mistake you can make in this class?"

Mark said, "Not doing the work."

"What if you know your story isn't great?"

Mark said, "That's progress."

"What if it is really embarrassingly bad?"

Mark said, "That's real progress."

"This class is about making art," the Professor said. "It's not designed to help you feel good about yourself. It's not yoga. It's not psychotherapy. In fact, you won't be allowed to speak when the rest of us talk about what you've written—and we will talk about every word you write. We will ignore you. We will refer to you not by name but as The Writer. In effect, you will not be here. You will be present solely in the words on your page. Just like real writers."

The time for dropping the class had come, and though several students picked up their coats and bags, they were only shopping for open spaces on the windowsills or the arm of someone else's chair. The Professor did take this opportunity to let Mark know he'd slightly altered the scenario for the first assignment yet again, so instead of distributing the second batch of thirty copies he'd typed up and printed, Mark found a pen to annotate as the Professor told the students to take careful notes.

There is a ~~man~~ woman in a room. There is a door, a window, and a chair in the room. ~~Another~~ A man comes to the door. He says, "We'll be with you in a few minutes. Don't open the window." He leaves. He returns. The window is open.

"Who is this woman?" the Professor asked. "Where is she?"

These were, by Mark's count, the first genuine questions the Professor had uttered. He wasn't surprised by the confusion they engendered. While half the students pretended to be still carefully writing out the scenario, the others were smiling politely, clearly expecting the Professor to bark out the answers to his own questions.

"It's not a riddle," Mark said. "There is no singular solution. She is a woman. Knowing only what you've been told, just tell the rest of us what her story is."

Someone at the back of the room said, "She's a patient of some kind."

Mark said, "I can hear you, but I can't see you. Do you have a name?"

The young woman knelt straight up. "I'm Willa." She tried to tuck her too-short brown hair behind her ears. "She's obviously a patient."

"I thought the guy was a doctor, too."

"Great," Mark said. "Do you come with a name?"

"Max." He was a lithe little white guy with a blond ponytail. He was wearing an expensive, oversized white shirt and a smirk.

"I think she's having an abortion." This was a small girl, her face mottled with freckles or acne.

Willa said, "That would make her a patient."

"She's a mental patient." This was a big guy with dark hair in the chair nearest Mark's. "I'm Julio. That's why there's no furniture in there, right?"

Another guy said, "There's a chair."

"I bet she jumps." This young man was a silhouette in one of the bright windows. "That's what the guy was afraid of, the doctor, why he told her not to open it."

Willa said, "Then why put her in a room with a window in the first place?"

"He could be a dentist." This was Anton.

A woman next to him said, "He could be a nurse."

Mark said, "Show of hands. How many people imagine this woman is in a medical or psychiatric facility of some kind—that she is in some kind of trouble and needs help?"

All but two of the students raised a hand. One young man thought she was applying for a job, another was still pretending to be occupied with writing out the assignment.

The Professor said, "Based on what? I said nothing about doctors or hospitals or illness. So what about the scenario suggested what you imagined? And why did so many of you all have the same associations with that woman and that room?"

After a few silent seconds, Mark stood up and said, "It's a genuine question." He turned to the blackboard behind his chair and picked up a piece of chalk. "Somebody start."

When the flood of responses finally died down, Mark stepped away from the board and admired what they had done.

Room
bare/impersonal/clinical/cold/no decorations/no amenities

Man
gives orders/can come and go as he pleases/uses Royal We/speaks in short sentences/ doesn't say please/offers no explanations

Woman
alone/given orders/forced to wait/never speaks/no name/disobedient

Literal Text
short sentences/simple vocabulary/staccato rhythm/no extraneous details/ all facts, no feelings/no adverbs/no adjectives

The Professor said, "Every word matters." This was the fundamental lesson of the day. He pointed out how that single pronoun—*we*—altered our sense of a man, his role, and an entire situation. Syntax—the structure of sentences, their length, and their relative complexity or simplicity—affected not only the pace and tone of the literal text but the atmosphere and mood of the setting and relationships. Details apparently as insignificant as furniture—items that were named, and those that were not—assumed suggestive significance. "So each one must be chosen, and each chosen one must be a telling detail. You haven't the time or space to furnish an entire room for readers. Leave to the reader what the reader can do for herself. But be specific enough to lead the reader. One detail changes everything. How different your impressions of this woman would be if I had put her in a recliner. Or a throne." He paused to let that sink in.

Willa said, "The man would become her servant."

Some guy at the back said, "You wish."

"He could be her financial adviser." This was a woman wearing a sage-green headscarf. "Or her husband, or—I'm Rashid, by the way, or are we not still doing that?"

The Professor said, "Rashid. So noted."

"The point is," Rashid said, a little tartly, "he could be anyone."

"But he must not be," the Professor said. "In your story, he must be someone." He enumerated several basic techniques for establishing a character's identity and role, along with a few of the common ways opening paragraphs mislead readers. Typically, Mark would have been outlining all of this on the blackboard, but he'd noticed there was a student perched on the arm of every chair, in addition to the students in those chairs, and the twelve-thirteen-fourteen-fifteen crammed into the windowsills, and there were at least half a dozen more on the floor. He doubted his math and started again, but when he saw Anton in a chair and on a windowsill, and then counted two sage-scarved women, he stopped, sat down and closed his eyes for a moment.

"My name is Penelope," said a woman with black bangs. "I'm wondering why so many of us thought that woman was troubled, or in trouble."

"That's a rich question for a literary critic," the Professor said. "The question for the writer is, How should that response from readers inform my choices? Every reader brings a host of inherited stories, as well as a vast array of associations with diction, syntax, and even punctuation. We have to learn how to use all of the material every reader brings—either to confirm that reader's sense or to unsettle and complicate it." The Professor paused and nodded ponderously, and Mark knew he was contemplating an impromptu syllabus revision, probably involving a quick Q&A about that woman in the room to dispense with the first writing assignment—which did often produce some tedious stories—and effectively negate Mark's lesson plans for the next two classes.

The Professor had done this more than a few times, never to good effect, but even disastrous results had not cured him. It was a tic, doubting Mark, rethinking Mark, attempting to revise Mark—not the Professor's most endearing quality, but this time Mark was prepared. He slapped one hand on the table, then the other, and then kept this up for a while. He asked the students to close their eyes.

Mark said, "We've all seen this movie." He continued the slapping. "This is in answer to your question, Penelope. There is a woman walking on a dark city street. Behind her, you hear this—footfalls." He increased the pace of the slapping. "No one among us thinks, Something wonderful is about to happen to her." He stood up. "How predictable women are. Such troubling, troubled creatures. Now, open your eyes. How many of you imagined that when the man returned to the room with the open window that the woman had jumped?"

More than half of the hands in the class went up.

Mark smiled. "Does that tell us something about this woman or about us?"

"Don't answer that," the Professor said. "Your job is to write her story."

Mark said, "It is due on Monday at 8:00 a.m. in my email box."

"We're running late, and it's only the first day," the Professor said. "One final note from me. If you decide to drop this class and you are registered or on the official wait list, it will serve your fellow students greatly if you go to StudentServe and delete your name. And only the stories written by the officially registered twelve will receive responses."

"On a happier note," Mark said, "let me read out the Technical Limits for your story."

1. No more than 250 words. Along with your name, please put the word count on your story.
2. Past tense.
3. Third-person narration. The perspective can be limited or omniscient, and don't worry if you don't understand the distinction, which we will review and discuss later in class. The idea is simply to use the convention of a narrator who is not a character in the story.

He paused just long enough for a few students to cap their pens. "Oh, yes. And one more limit: Use only monosyllabic words." He paused again. "Really."

The predictable moment of stillness and silence gave way to smiles as everyone packed up bags and zippered parkas. The fuse had been lit. A woman said, "Monosyllabic? You mean one syllable? Only one syllable?"

Another woman said, "That rules out *woman*."

Julio said, "What about *window*? Or even *open*?"

The room exploded with shouted words and moaning and laughter and questions, and above the din, Mark heard Anton yell, "I'm so screwed," as his yellow sweater flashed by and out the door, and by the time Mark had done what he could to assuage the anxious and reassure the dubious, committed a few more names to memory, promised to meet with eight students who were certain they would not be among the lucky twelve but wanted to write the first story anyway, the Professor had disappeared, so Mark patted the back of his empty chair and said, "Here we go again."

5.

Mark didn't go back to his office. He headed straight for the garage, skidding across the frozen pond past three young men and a woman, all wearing

Toronto Maple Leafs jerseys, who were deeply disappointed that he was not a late-arriving recruit for the Curling Club.

"Give it a try," one of them called out. "It's fun."

"Not as much fun as teaching," he said. It was a reflex, a thoughtless comment that surprised Mark as thoroughly as it confounded the curlers. But he meant it. Which was really why he was avoiding Hum Hall today. He didn't want to entertain the griping and grousing of colleagues beset by the end of their six-week winter break. Mark sped off campus toward Ipswich to preserve his good mood—and his pride. In the last few years, he'd begun to be embarrassed by the unalloyed joy he felt in the classroom, which he had too often copped to in public. His preference not to sound like an idiot accounted for the dwindling of his social contact with colleagues and his particular efforts to avoid casual conversations with the Professor, who had mentioned after a dinner with alums last semester that Mark's rapturous description of the workshops had made Mark sound like an idiot.

About four miles shy of his house, Mark had a dispiriting thought: NEPCAJE. He glanced hopefully at his black bag on the passenger seat, and then turned and hopelessly scanned the back seat, and then he exited off Route 1 North and looped back to Route 1 South toward campus to retrieve the books, which he needed to write a draft of the literature review for the New England Private College Access, Justice, and Excellence initiative. He had four free days ahead, and he knew he'd never get to the task once students started delivering their stories.

A few miles later, he also knew he wouldn't get back to Hum Hall through the snarled-up commuter traffic for at least an hour.

Against his better judgment, he dug out his phone. Safety was not a concern—traffic was barely moving, and the melodramatic Saab coughed and sighed every time he released the clutch, threatening to expire. It was his mood that was at risk again. And when he read the first of many texts from Paul—*Finally in Rome!*—his spirits wavered.

He didn't want to be in Rome, but he didn't want Paul to be there, either. He didn't want to crawl back to campus, but he didn't want to be at home alone, either. So, he slipped the phone into his bag and nosed his car into the breakdown lane, where he sped along to the next exit and pointed his reluctant Saab toward Cambridge, and the spartan luxury of Paul's condo.

When Paul was at home, there was little evidence of normal human habitation between the white walls of his one-bedroom condo. But before he'd gone away, he'd even removed his vast collection of unsalted nuts in Mason jars from the counter in the galley kitchen. Where he'd stashed them and the steel-cut oatmeal, quinoa, and flaxseeds was almost as mysterious as why he ingested so much indigestible stuff. After Mark had admired the segregated suits and starched shirts in the bedroom closet and nosed around in the neat stack of new magazines beside the sofa in the living room, he studied the two bathrobes on the hook on the back of the bathroom door and opted not for his Medium but the Large—Paul's. That helped. Feeling happily at home, he sat in the old club chair Paul kept by the windows in his living room to read through the rest of the text messages from Rome.

The Paean Project had secured Paul a big studio apartment with a little balcony overlooking the Piazza Navona. This also helped. Years ago, they'd spent a week in Rome and squandered a lot of time together admiring Bernini's superb Fountain of Four Rivers and everything they ate in the cafés lining that piazza. This made it easy for Mark to eclipse the time until spring break and imagine himself on that wrought iron balcony. And then he read that Paul was flying to Greece in the morning to spend three days at a refugee-processing camp on Lesbos. *And then maybe two days in Tunis?*

Mark stopped reading and stared out at the paths winding through the patchy snow on the Cambridge Common and the red taillights of cars winding through Harvard Square. Beyond that, the visible earth tipped out of view but for the gleam of Boston across the Charles River and the very top of the Hancock Tower, whose weather-predicting spire was blinking blue, promising a sunny tomorrow. But forecasting the future was a dicey proposition. Had Mark ditched his class this semester and gone to Rome to be with Paul, he wouldn't be with him tomorrow.

In a final blast of brief messages, Paul let Mark know he wasn't sure if or when he'd be able to be in touch over the weekend, and his last text was, *What have I got myself into?*

Mark wrote, *The world,* and hit send. It was already nearly midnight in Rome, and he knew Paul would be asleep, so instead of calling, he typed again. *And the world is lucky to have you. Call when you can. Wherever you are, you're here, too.*

Mark's mood was heading downhill, but it got waylaid by three loud raps on the back door, and then three more. The back door was only two feet from the front door, but Mark knew he didn't have a visitor. The knocks were a code. He pulled his wool cap from the sleeve of his parka and fished through his bag for a lighter, but came up empty. He climbed up the stairs to the roof, where no one was allowed. The steel door was propped open with a shovel, and a path had been cleared through the snow to the make-shift deck of plywood pallets outfitted with two plastic Adirondack chairs and a bucket of sand.

Dennis Blake didn't turn around right away. From the back, he was just a careless wave of blondish hair atop a handsome camel hair coat, a pair of un-laced construction boots, and a couple of bare calves. Dennis billed himself as a real-estate developer, though the only property he owned was this five-story brick building—or a lot of it. Since his wife had inherited it from her father about twenty years ago, Dennis had been slowly selling off the rental units on the first two floors. Paul lived on the top floor, and he and one other long-time renter up there had been allowed to buy their units, but Dennis had combined the other eight apartments on the fifth floor into his home, office, gym, and a projection room from which he monitored the many cameras he'd installed in the lobby, halls, elevator, and stairways. Diana Blake was a child psychologist, which was the best explanation for her enduring attachment to Dennis, who suddenly turned around with his hands in his coat pockets to make it clear he was wearing only boxer shorts and a white hoodie underneath.

"Professor!"

Even students rarely addressed Mark by this title, so it always occasioned a momentary confusion.

"Welcome back!" Dennis backed up two steps and, imitating the quarterback he probably was in high school, tossed a pack of American Spirits to Mark. "Keep them. I quit for the New Year."

"So did I," Mark said. He had sworn off smoking in his house years ago, swore it off on campus last year, and this year he'd added his car to the forbidden list, so he was more often than not not smoking. "Got a light?"

As he approached, Dennis said, "I thought Paul left for Rome a week ago."

"He came to Ipswich for a few days and left—" Mark cupped his hands and would have tipped his head toward the flame in Dennis's left hand, but Dennis had helpfully placed his right hand on the back of Mark's head to save him the effort. Mark wasn't sure if he was being offered a light or what was half hidden beneath Dennis's boxer shorts, and when he took a long pull on the cigarette and said, "Paul left for Rome from Ipswich this morning," Dennis didn't immediately pull away.

With one hand massaging Mark's neck, Dennis stuck his other hand into the pocket of Mark's robe. "Keep the lighter. Until we meet again. Jesus!" He stepped back and wagged his head back and forth. "You smell good. What are you wearing?"

"Paul's bathrobe," Mark said.

"Figures," Dennis said as he retreated to his chair. "I meant to give him that book about Teddy Roosevelt before he left. Did he tell you Diana is pregnant? He didn't leave his car on the street, did he? Get me the keys and I'll pull it into one of our spaces till he gets back. I'm making a nursery for a goddess downstairs. You guys gotta come see it when it's done."

All of this was well within the normal range in Dennis World. Just when you thought you had a handle on him—illiterate, selfish, bisexual, boor— he said something else that forced you to reconsider. They each smoked two cigarettes, and Mark guessed Dennis's weight incorrectly (twice—both times too high, which made Dennis question his new diet), and then to make amends, Mark pointed out the Winter Triangle of Sirius, Betelgeuse, and Procyon in the southeastern sky.

Dennis whistled something that sounded a lot like "Taps."

Mark closed his eyes, and after a few moments of silence, he said, "This is like being on a cruise ship."

"Yeah, or a drive-in." Dennis was bent over the bucket of sand, arranging three of their spent filters into a triangle. He flicked the other one to-ward the Common, and Mark mentioned that Paul had let a friend borrow his car while he was away, and then they went downstairs, back to being nonsmokers.

After he made a couple of aimless circuits around Paul's place, Mark found a love letter from Paul in the refrigerator—two half gallons of orange juice, two half gallons of whole milk, and two pounds of Colombian coffee. Toss in the takeout menu from Dumpling Empire and the flat-screen TV in Paul's bedroom, and you had the recipe for a recluse.

6.

By 8:00 a.m. on Monday, Mark had consumed two Peking ducks, more than a dozen home-renovation programs, four orders of sesame noodles, the bet-ter parts of six men's and four women's tennis matches at small-tournament warm-ups for the imminent Australian Open, eighteen dumplings, a lot of garlicky greens, and with the assistance of a fresh pot brewed from the second pound of Colombian coffee, he'd downloaded the stories students had dutifully delivered to his email box, segregated the submissions from registered students into a file for the Professor, and finally persuaded Paul's printer to make copies of everything so he could read through the lot before class. He'd ventured outside seven times, if only up and out with Dennis, who had knocked more than a dozen times over the weekend and, instead of acting annoyed or insulted when his rapping was ignored, congratulated Mark on quitting so often.

Nineteen students turned up for Monday's class, and after the Pro-fessor assured them that the twelve registered students had submitted sto-ries so the enrollment was settled, two guys packed up and left. With his long and unpleasant preview of the grammar lesson Mark was about to conduct "for those of you who missed this in third grade," the Professor might have scared away two or three others. Mark distrusted his most recent head count, as he'd spotted Anton, Willa, and Julio twice, and

Penelope might have been on a windowsill and in the chair below it, and unless there were two women wearing ice-blue headscarves, he'd seen two Rashids, as well.

"Despite what you may have heard, everything you need to know about English grammar is regular, reliable, and remarkably elegant," Mark said, turning to the blackboard and urging everyone to take notes. "We're not going to unravel all of your confusion or anticipate every question that might arise later in the semester, but you are going to leave today knowing absolutely everything you need to know to write perfect and perfectly grammatical sentences for the rest of your lives." He skipped his usual invitation of interruptions and questions, hoping to speed through the necessaries, hand out the packets of twelve stories he'd printed and collated and stapled, and then get somewhere quiet with a large bottle of fizzy water.

His entire lecture could be boiled down to two distinctions. The first was a *phrase* (a series of related words with no specific grammatical function, such as *the red hat, last night,* or *forever and a day*) versus a *clause* (a group of words that included a noun and a related verb). The Professor said, "Subject and predicate."

Mark said, "Or in English, a noun and related verb. And you need only worry over two kinds of clauses." This was the key distinction.

The Professor said, "Insubordinate and subordinate."

Mark said, "Translation? The independent clause and the dependent clause," and then wrote on the board, *The boy cried. The girl left.* "Those are both independent—they can stand alone as complete sentences. In fact, they are perfect sentences. Elegant—the sort of simple, declarative sentences that English is designed to produce. And here's the thing for every writer to remember: every English sentence must contain one independent clause."

When he saw a couple of hands shoot up, he pretended not to notice and wrote, *After the boy cried. By the time the girl left.* Keeping his back to the class, he said, "These are dependent clauses—dependent on more information. And if you will tolerate a moment's confusion, we'll start by defining the dependent clause as an independent clause preceded by a dependent

word or phrase. Typically, those are prepositions or prepositional phrases."
He wrote *pre-position*. "You see? Words or phrases that establish place in
time or space."

The Professor said, "Prepositions are more complex than just that."

"But that's a proposition we can entertain later in the semester if there
is a contingent of aspiring linguists or lexicographers in the group," said
Mark. "For writers, it's enough to know that, by itself, a dependent clause
is a fragment. Perpetually incomplete. And no matter how many dependent
clauses you string together, you don't have a sentence until you write one
entirely independent clause."

Someone yelled, "Can a sentence have more than one independent
clause?"

"Yes. And right on cue. The trick is coordination." Mark erased everything on the board and wrote quickly. "For starters, here are two problems
you've heard about before, I'm sure." He stepped aside.

Run-on sentence: The girl laughed the boy cried.

A run-on, he explained, was not a long sentence or even a too-long
sentence. It was simply uncoordinated independent clauses. And putting a
comma between independent clauses just created another problem.

Comma splice: The girl laughed, the boy cried.

"An English sentence might arrive with one or one hundred independent clauses, and one hundred dependent clauses or none. But it won't reliably take readers where you want them to go if you don't coordinate those
clauses." He turned back to the board and wrote as he spoke. "To coordinate
two independents you need a comma and a conjunction"—

The boy cried, and the girl left. The boy cried, but the girl left.

—"or you have to make one clause dependent."

When the boy cried, the girl left. The boy cried after the girl left.

Penelope—the Penelope on the windowsill—asked why there was no
comma in the second example.

"I had a superb teacher in third grade," Mark said. "She asked us to
memorize two sentences, which I am now asking you to write down exactly
as I say them." Pronouncing not only the words but the punctuation, he

slowly said, "When the dependent clause comes first, you need a comma. You need no comma when the independent clause comes first."

Someone yelled, "Holy shit."

The Professor shouted, "Max!"

"No. That was me. I'm Isaac."

Isaac was seated in the chair nearest the front of the room. Mark fixed his gaze on him to avoid the eyes of the guy seated on the sill directly behind Isaac. Both of them were wearing Maple Leafs hockey jerseys, both with a bold number 14.

The Professor said, "For starters, it is *I. I spoke. Me* had nothing to do with it."

The Isaac in the chair said, "I'm so sorry I cursed. It's just amazing to realize how far I've gotten without understanding how to write a simple sentence."

Max said, "Yeah, me feels like an idiot, too."

A woman near the back added, "While you were saying that—comma—we were all thinking the same thing."

This was the perfect last note for the day, and if Mark had not glanced at his watch to confirm that there was still half an hour of class time in the bank, that woman might have had the last word. Instead, the Professor said, "And now, let me add a few items to your notes that are not rules but useful tips. For starters, when do you absolutely need to use a semicolon in your fiction?"

Mark sat down and said, "Never."

The Professor said, "When should you use a semicolon in fiction?"

Mark said, "Never."

There was a long litany of unnecessary punctuation, from exclamation points to ellipses—and a longer series of tips that kept the students busy taking notes for about twenty minutes. The gist of the Professor's jumble of advice, warnings, biases, and opinions was simple—rely on conventions, eliminate devices. When he finished, he pulled a sheet of paper from the top of the pile of collated stories and read. "Dorothy, Mark, Max, Isaac, Rashid, Jane, Penelope, Julio, Charles, Willa, Virginia, and Leo. Those are the lucky twelve whose stories are in the packet for Wednesday. They constitute the workshop. Their assignment is to read all twelve stories carefully, which is to say, at least twice."

No one moved. Mark said, "I will be in my office from one till three on Wednesday, happy to meet with anyone whose name was not called. If you email me in advance, I'll have read and thought about the story you wrote. The other twelve, please take a packet on your way out." Still no one moved.

The Professor said, "Now, go away."

And they did, eventually, all of them, including the look-alikes, to Mark's relief—everybody but Anton, who stayed in his chair midway down the long table. He was wearing the yellow V-neck again, and though he'd found a long blue and yellow scarf to wind around his neck, he hadn't yet acquired a hat or coat.

Mark said, "Please tell me you've got a parka stuffed in your knapsack."

"I'll tell you anything you want to hear if you let me into this class."

"That's not up to me, Anton."

"I know it's on me, but I am a senior." He waited to see if this news altered his status. "And not only that, I've been a senior for about eighteen months. I need this."

Mark said, "There are other English courses, and other writing workshops."

"No, I mean this course is exactly what I need. I could take any course for graduation credits. That's not the point." He smiled sadly, and then turned away and stared out the window behind his chair for a long time. "This is a good room, isn't it?"

"Feels real," Mark said.

"Like a real college, you mean?"

That was exactly what Mark meant. "Whatever that might be."

Anton stood up and leaned back against that window. "I think it's like this—college is, when it's real. How we feel in this class. You gotta let me in, Mark—if it really is okay to call you that."

Mark said, "That's my name."

"I'm probably a lousy writer, and I can't really remember if I've ever written a whole story—I mean one I made up. Do you know what time it is?"

"About a quarter to five."

"Phew. I am on the wait list, somewhere near the top, and I know at least one of those guys who didn't stay for your grammar thing was ahead of me. So." Anton uncoiled his scarf about halfway, and then wound it back up. "I have an appointment at five thirty. I changed them all so I won't have to leave class early ever again."

It was Anton's *ever* that got to Mark, as if he'd understood that time with anyone anywhere was infinite and circumscribed. It certainly made Mark's standard speech about the college's commitment to small classes and the democratic selection process seem inane. "It's just not up to me, Anton."

"Something happened in the first class, and it happened to me again today." He paused and tugged at the ends of his scarf. "I don't even know how to describe it."

"Whatever it is, it's not about this particular room, or how I happen to—"

"That's not what I'm talking about."

"I know," Mark said, though he was not sure he did. And though he could already feel his ears ringing with the Professor's protestations, above that din he could still hear Anton's *ever*. "When does the Drop-Add period end?"

Anton said, "A week or two."

Mark said, "So, not for another two or three classes."

"So, I'll see you on Wednesday?" Anton retrieved his bag from the table. "Should I make copies of the story I wrote?"

"I can do that," Mark said. "And no guarantees. But stay on the wait list."

Anton shoved in each chair he passed on his way to the door. "I meant what I said—about me maybe being a lousy writer."

Mark said, "My being."

Anton said, "My being?"

"Your being," Mark said.

"This stuff is fantastic," Anton said, and then he disappeared.

7.

Before he left campus, Mark went to his office and dutifully pulled off his shelves all of the books he'd been assigned to review for the New England Private College Access, Justice, and Excellence initiative. After trying and failing to stuff them into his bag, he found an empty recycling bin in the hall, dumped in the books, and headed for Ipswich. He spent most of Monday night and all of the weirdly warm and rainy Tuesday morning hoping for three things—an update from Paul, the Professor's responses to the first set of stories, and some mention of classrooms in the critiques of higher education on the NEPCAJE reading list. He'd prompted Paul with two emails, several texts, and pictures of the snowless deck, roof, and driveway of the Ipswich house under the heading, "Global Warming: The Benefits." Still, no word from wherever he was. And nothing from the Professor by noon. This was unusual. The Professor typically didn't devote a lot of time to the first Technical Exercise, as he figured that most of the students would not choose to revise those monosyllabic stories for their final portfolios. He was typically proved right. The Professor considered this a reflection on Mark's assignment. Mark considered it a reflection of the shock and shame students experienced when they read the Professor's comments and realized someone was treating every word they'd written as if it meant something, or ought to.

At the end of their first semester together at Hellman, Mark had attempted and failed to persuade the Professor to try his hand at the Technical Exercises. According to the Professor, the classroom was a sacred space— those were his words—where twelve undergraduates could be transformed into writers, and unfashionable as it was to invoke the power of ritual and religion, someone had to be the priest, someone who believed in the possibility of transubstantiation. Mark wondered if that meant he was the Professor's altar boy—he'd done some time in a cassock and surplice as a kid. The Professor rather dismissively reminded Mark that he was an adult. He should do what he had to do.

So Mark took to writing a new story to fulfill each Technical Exercise every semester. In deference to the Professor, he never showed these to the students. All Mark asked was that the Professor always read his story first. Mark didn't know if his efforts made the Professor more mindful of how challenging the assignments were. But he liked to think that he was an effective sacrificial lamb. The Professor's responses to the students' stories were still comprehensive, blunt, astute, and unnerving, but not dispiriting, not deadly. He had a poison tongue, the Professor, but these days he lavished most of his venom on Mark.

On this dreary Tuesday, however, it was Anton and his comment about their classroom that preoccupied Mark as he migrated with his books from the dining room that was his study to a stool in the kitchen overlooking the deck, down to Paul's desk in the guest room, which was outfitted with a stationary bicycle that moved only when Paul dutifully climbed aboard. Mark's house was small—something less than 750 square feet of marginally habitable space—but it offered a surprising number of alternative places to read and write and think, which suited his peripatetic habit of mind. Built as a one-room tavern—now, the living room and kitchen on the main floor—the verifiably Colonial portion had been wheeled on logs from downtown and shoved into the side of a little hill above the Ipswich River in the early 1800s. That must have been when the owner decided that the profoundly eaved attic was a plausible bedroom. About a hundred years later, someone built a two-story ten-by-ten box and nailed it to the back wall of the kitchen to create a tiny bathroom and dining room on the main floor and a biggish room of indeterminate purpose below, abutting the dirt-floored cellar. Mark had added a bathroom in the attic, and then another bathroom so the indeterminate ground-floor space could serve as a guest bedroom and a quiet space for Paul to work. All of this fiddling by generations of carpenters as intrepid and ill-trained as Mark had resulted in a structure that perfectly resembled a tipsy sheet cake with three layers, each a different length, held together by icing and toothpicks.

During the first winter in the house, Paul had mentioned several times that it was cool at his desk downstairs, even after Mark repeatedly jacked up the thermostat in the living room and strategically positioned fans at the top of the attic and basement stairs to spread the wealth more equitably. He finally broke down and called a licensed plumber, a big guy with a belly that had to be helped around the furniture while he inspected the tiny dining room and the guest room below. Finally, he asked if Mark had noticed the baseboards in those rooms were cold to the touch.

Mark hadn't.

"That's because there aren't any," the plumber said. "Whoever built this addition didn't add heat. I can do that, but you might want to get a carpenter in here, as well." This guy wasn't an architect, but he was wearing overalls, which gave him an air of authority. "Have you noticed these rooms sort of slant away from the rest of your house?"

Mark assured him he had noticed that, making it clear the heating oversight was an anomaly. "It's an old structure," he added, with a knowing shrug.

"It's gonna be two structures pretty soon if you don't get someone in here to hang a beam and properly attach these rooms to the rest of this little birdhouse," the plumber said.

By the end of that spring, there was heat for Paul, a beam to bring things back together, and a deck off the kitchen with a three-season porch below, where Mark finally landed on Tuesday evening with the NEPCAJE books. He could squeeze a fourth season out of the unheated porch if he wore a parka, bathrobe, and a beanie and sat near the exterior wall of the house, which leaked plenty of heat. After several hours of reading the new student stories and responding to emails, if he squinted he could still squeeze enough light out of the overhead lamp to read another chapter from one of the NEPCAJE tomes. But he could squeeze almost nothing about classrooms or teaching from that pile of books documenting the various crises in higher education.

Mark's assignment was to write a summary of what was in those books, but all he'd achieved was a comprehensive survey of what was not in those books. He had flagged two lists. The first was Ten Habits of Highly Successful Teachers. By his quick count, he and the Professor together exhibited exactly none of them, and the Professor had explicit policies that were diametrically opposed to at least seven of the strategies and attitudes of their successful counterparts. The second list enumerated elements of Poisonous Pedagogy: Killing Creativity. Mark was confident he and the Professor could be convicted on several counts of toxic teaching for their murderous approach to creativity, but instead he turned his attention to the Professor's responses to the first set of student stories.

Mark Sternum/Technical Exercise 1.

This is a genuinely engaging and intriguing first draft, and you handle the monosyllabic diction with apparent ease. In several sequences here, the clipped diction generates a gratifyingly swift pace, which gives us a clear sense of both Paul's haste and Mark's lethargy. (Your original assignment did involve two men. But in the final version, it was a woman in that room. If you write your story before the students write theirs, to prove it can be done, you might as well write a story that embraces the Technical Limits in the actual assignment.)

As it is, my principal question about this draft is the point of view—and whether you might reconsider your choice. Early on, I assumed I was limited to the Paul character, though it later became evident that I was also receiving information (Paul's coat flying by the bed) from Mark's point of view. But the story never makes full use of the omniscience. On second reading, I wondered if this might be a stronger (and more emotionally coherent) story if the narration gave us only Paul's point of view. (Mark's perspective seems irrelevant—technically of no real significance. Plus, his behavior marks him as a kind of man-child, self-indulgent and more than a little annoying. Intentional?)

This, of course, is most pertinent in the final sequence, where I do too often feel the hand of the writer. I wonder initially about Paul's impatience—but given who he is stuck with, I do buy it in

Technical Exercise 1.

(Mark Sternum / 250 words)

The door hinge creaked. Paul leaned in, grabbed his coat from the old club chair. "It's eight."

Mark groaned from the bed. "Come here."

"I'm late," Paul said.

"I said I'd make poached eggs."

"That was at six." Cold air streamed toward Paul like a tide.

Mark watched the tails of Paul's tweed coat fly by the bed.

Paul reached for the pane Mark had raised. "I told you to keep this closed."

"I told you not to take the gig in Rome."

Paul's hands drooped to the sill. "You said you'd take this spring term off."

"Did I?"

"Don't start." Paul turned to Mark. "Don't you teach soon?"

"Not till three."

"I should have stayed at my place." Paul pulled a Swiss knife from his coat, aimed the blade at the track.

Mark sat up. "I'll close that."

"It takes two—the track's bent." Paul huffed out a sigh. "I hate to rouse you, but my ride is here."

Mark joined Paul, saw the sleek black cab by the snow bank.

Paul said, "Grab the frame. On three, shut it. One, two—"

"Five months?"

"Three." Paul pulled the knife out, but Mark failed to slam down the pane.

The cab beeped twice.

They watched it drive off down the street.

"My bad," Mark said. "Spring Break in Rome?"

"It's too late for this."

"I mean it."

Paul said, "So do I," and shoved Mark out, watched him fall to the ground. Mark just could not keep it closed.

Comment [m1]: Stories typically arrive with titles.

Comment [m2]: Terrific sequence. We get a clear sense both of Paul's directness and Mark's fantastic lassitude. I'm all for the streaming air – a useful suggestion of the window being open, and it clarifies the back story about Paul having told Mark not to open the window. However, *toward* has two syllables. (Look it up.) You could use "streamed *by*" or "streamed *past*."

Comment [m3]: At this point, I wonder about the ages of these guys and how long they've been a couple. Maybe it's a tone problem? (Is the clipped diction meant to suggest genuine impatience or familiarity? Unclear.)

Comment [m4]: Should I understand why Mark opened the window? (I don't.)

Comment [m5]: Or, simply, Paul sighed.

Comment [m6]: The numerical confusion is lovely and feels organic – unlike the two residences, which feels imported. (And weird.)

Comment [m7]: On my first reading, I didn't buy this murder. On second reading, I wanted to murder Mark, and this outré gesture seemed oddly plausible. But I do wonder, again, why we are not limited to Paul. We don't need Mark's point of view to understand the action.

the end. But Mark's stasis, and his sophomoric way of taking the blame ("My bad.") without accepting responsibility (still, he does nothing to remedy the situation he has caused) feels scripted, not lived. Or maybe that final sequence leaves me with too many unanswered questions about what, exactly, Mark understands is at stake in this moment. It occurred to me that Mark actually regretted being awakened. (Can that be the truth about him?)

I do see how the disparity in maturity between the two men and the bugsomeness of the Mark character can reasonably account for the rather dramatic ending. But the oddball detail about Paul not living in the same house as his lover is complicating my reading of the final moments of the story. You might try to rework that element—it is a peculiar way for adults to conduct an intimate relationship, and though it does underscore the idea that Paul is wisely hedging his bets in the relationship, if Paul actually lived with Mark—had been genuinely committed to him—it might be easier to earn the ending you were aiming for here.

You've done the hard work of making us believe in the open window—that one adult had asked that it remain closed, and another adult had ignored that request. That's great narrative work. Now, the challenge as you revise is to make the nature of their relationship clearer (more credible?) so we have a better purchase on the emotional stakes. I mean, what exactly does Mark want that explains his oversleeping and his reluctance to get out of bed on the morning his partner is leaving the country for several months? And Paul—what's in it for him when the story begins? Why does he bother to wake Mark? Paul seems entirely reasonable and—well, adult. Does he really want nothing more than to see that window closed? Or should we sense from the start that Paul is itching to get away from Mark—not for a few months, but once and for all?

TWO

Technical Exercise 2.
(Mark Sternum / 250 words: Part I 183/Part II 67)

At midnight, my phone rings, and Anton giddily announces he's outside in a pickup, so I grab my parka, but he won't lower his window, forcing me into the passenger seat, and he floors it, squeals past a stop sign, and soon we're sailing down icy curves to the beach, and maybe because he's wearing sunglasses, I announce I can't joyride with my student, and he says he's not anymore, his parents cut him off and he got a job plowing snow, but don't worry, he whispers, rubbing my thigh, he'll be back next semester, and then a reflective yellow vest catches the headlights, and the pickup clips the jogger, slams her into the pavement, blood spilling from her misshapen skull as Anton skids to a stop, hyperventilating, and when I open my door, he confesses he's fucked up and carrying, pulls a pipe from his pocket as proof and defeatedly folds the sunglasses into their protective case, so I glance at the woman—the corpse—and the dark, dark road ahead and order Anton to pull a U-turn and follow my directions.

Anton disappears, as instructed. The case goes unsolved for a blessed month, and then a horn honks during a snowstorm. Anton's pickup is sporting a plow attachment.

He rolls down his window. "After you convinced me to drive away." His eyes are bloodshot.

"What?"

"It's a dependent clause. Unfinished." Anton slams down the plow blade, revealing his pickup's mangled front end.

A neighbor's porch light flips on.

* * *

1.

It was nearly noon on Wednesday when Mark finally finished revising his story to conform to the limits of Technical Exercise 2. This was the Professor's favorite of all the exercises Mark had dreamed up, and it was a safe bet he wouldn't alter the scenario before class, so Mark printed out copies of the assignment for the workshop and then topped off his coffee, lit a cigarette, and settled back into his perch at the edge of the kitchen counter.

Along with the assignment for this new story, the students would receive the comments from the Professor on their first stories in class today, and Mark worried as he did at the start of every semester that the sting of the Professor's remarks about those open-window stories wouldn't fade. They probably wouldn't, but surely neither would his praise. Everything meant so much to the Professor.

Mark knew his use of Anton in the new story was a risk. And he was confident the Professor would have something snide to say about the suggestion of seduction. But he wasn't sure how the Professor would respond to the story's suggestion that excluding Anton from the workshop on the basis of an arbitrary numerical limit could have unforeseen and dire consequences.

Mark had devoted four hours to his Anton story, and he'd meticulously observed the assignment's Technical Limits, but until he read the Professor's comments, he wouldn't really know what he had done.

Outside, the sun silvered the weather-beaten deck boards, promising an early spring, which promised Paul's return, which promised another summer, and as his spirits rose, so did the smoke, which accumulated like clouds on the ceiling and soon drifted down as fog, dragging Mark's mood with it.

How quickly he'd adjusted to Paul being gone, how thoughtlessly he'd lifted the in-house smoking ban, how readily he'd adapted to the expectation that Paul would not come sniffing around tonight or tomorrow. He ran some cold water and doused the cigarette, watching the wormy remains droop and disintegrate into the porcelain sink. To that squalid mess, he added the bowl of sodden cereal he'd abandoned hours earlier, and as the mound of flaccid flakes and swollen raisins drooled toward the drain he reminded himself that his sink, unlike Paul's, was not equipped with a garbage disposal. So, while Paul pulled North African refugees onshore to safety, Mark plucked raisins from the basket and strainer in his kitchen sink.

The Saab complained all the way to campus, something about its front end and potholes. Mark countered that noise with a radio broadcast of a White House press briefing staged to retract and reiterate the lies tweeted out overnight by the president. The emotional effort required to believe the country could survive Trump was just about equal to the self-deception involved in speeding down Route 1 in a collection of aftermarket parts slapped onto a rusty chassis manufactured by a car company that had gone bust.

Mark was already twenty minutes late for office hours when he got to the garage, so he left the recycling box full of NEPCAJE books in the back seat and vowed to devote Thursday and Friday, and the better part of the weekend, to those antimagnetic tomes about teaching. When he got to the second floor of Hum Hall, three guys in parkas and gym shorts were huddling beside his office door. Before Mark said a word, the nearest one unfolded a Drop-Add form and said they were all seniors and had been trying to get into the workshop for four years.

Mark stuck his key in the door. "I didn't see you at the first two class meetings."

"I can explain." This was the shortest of the three, and he patted his pockets in search of something.

The third guy tipped his headphones off his ears. "We're desperate."

The thumping music got a nod of approval from the first guy, who was clearly in charge. "We're basically here to beg."

The short one said, "We're at your mercy, sir." He'd started to pump his fists like pistons in time with the music. Soon, the beat got to the hips and heads of the other two.

Mark said, "You're not getting into the class, but you'd make a great boy band."

"We can do that." This was the first guy, who sprang to attention. "We'll be your opening act for every class. Please, Professor? We've heard great stuff about you."

Mark opened his office door. "You can come in and finish your pitch, but the class is full. And the waitlist is full. And more than a dozen seniors who have attended both class meetings are already not getting in."

They did persist. After a round of introductions and a rambling complaint about the lack of creative outlets on campus, the lead guy finally explained their plight in two words. "Restoration Comedy." All three of them had signed up for that class to complete their Humanities requirement. "Not funny."

The short kid added his two cents. "Tragic mistake."

"Nice try," Mark said. "Not happening."

The music man flipped his headphones back into place.

The group spokesman said, "Foiled again," and led the other two down the hall to the next office door.

As Mark sat at his desk, a young woman poked her head in. He recognized her from class and ventured a guess. "Wendy?"

"Yes! Hello. Are you free?" She was wearing an ankle-length blue coat and a cowboy hat, and she immediately shrugged off a backpack that banged down like an anvil. "How are you?" She flipped off the hat and kicked it under the unoccupied chair next to Mark's desk.

Mark said, "I'm happy to see you."

This seemed to confuse her. She reached up and tugged at her hair, as if it were a curtain she could pull down over her shoulders. "I guess I'll just sit here? I don't know why I cut my hair. I'm in your creative-writing class. Is this an okay time to talk?"

"It's perfect," Mark said. She wasn't making much sense, but her voice had a flat Midwestern plainness that made everything she said seem reasonable.

"I guess I just wanted to say how much I am enjoying the course." She was still standing, still worrying at the ripples of brown hair that seemed to be pasted to her head and neck. "That's lame—exactly what I didn't want to say. One of my housemates gave me this creme to stop my hair from springing out, and now I feel like one of those ducklings. You know, the ones you see after an oil spill? I'm Willa, by the way. I'm usually not like this." She waved her hands around to make it clear she wasn't just talking about her hair.

Mark said, "I'm really happy to know the course is making sense to you."

By the time Willa sat down, she'd told Mark she was pre-med, had early acceptance to Johns Hopkins for the fall, was an only child, lived with five other seniors in a three-bedroom apartment with no stove, wasn't sure she wanted to be a doctor, her parents were divorced and both taught biology at the University of Kansas, and a chemistry professor had given her two electric hotplates to use until that no-good stove was repaired or replaced, which is why her bag was so heavy. "I guess I wanted to know if you think it's something about me, or it might be something else, like that instead of using traditional books, we just read what other kids in the class write for our assigned reading, maybe? Also, I guess I was wondering, do other kids talk to you about this? I mean, is this normal?"

Mark smiled. He had no idea what Willa was trying to ask.

"I'm sure they do." Willa performed a quick hair check. Verdict: not great. "It's just I want to be sure it's not just me, that I'm, you know, not freaking out or something. Like just now. I see myself saying, It's not just me, and I wonder why she—why I—didn't say, It's not just I. Because I is correct, right? Even though it sounds odd? But the point is—who is that looking at me and thinking about what I just said? The whole time I worked on my first story, it was just like that—that's what I wanted to ask you about. It's like I'm reading over my own shoulder. Do you think that's, I don't know, pretty normal for someone who hasn't done anything creative before?"

"I think medicine is creative," Mark said.

"Well, thanks, but not really. It's mostly been memorizing so far. Writing that first story felt much more—well, not the same."

"That's great." This seemed to relax her, so Mark carried on. "You're feeling what you're meant to feel. That was the spirit of the monosyllabic limit. To make you self-conscious, to make you think about every word you write. Does that make sense?"

Willa nodded. "Self-consciousness—but doubled. Right? I mean, literally times two. Or, squared, maybe."

Mark didn't say anything. He was recalling her first story, which they would talk about in class today. In Willa's imagination, the woman who'd been instructed not to open the window was a trainee at a fast-food restaurant, stuck in a tiny glass booth. "Here's what I know. You wrote a superb first story. I love that she opens that window, and all those cars zip into line before the manager has anyone at the grill to fill the orders."

"And *mic* was okay? I mean, would you consider that natural language? Am I loving the limits like you said we had to love them? Or would you say I was gaming the limits with a word like that?"

"People refer to microphones as *mics* all the time." To Mark's surprise, this seemed to satisfy Willa. She really was worried about one word. "*Mic* is a standard noun—as familiar as, say, *phone*. Right?"

A loud knock at the door brought Willa to her feet. "Telephone," she said. "Right. I mean, no one would say, 'Stop checking your telephone while I'm talking to you.'" As if she were at home, Willa opened the door and ushered in another student from the workshop.

"I can come back," he mumbled. He was memorable—a somber tow-head who always pushed his chair back a few feet from the table, keeping his distance from most of what went on in class. He was wearing a puffy white ski parka bedizened with about $5,000 worth of lift tickets.

Before Mark could speak, Willa had shoved her backpack into the hall. "Your turn in the chair," she said as she returned to collect her hat and coat, and then she hollered, "See you both in class," and slammed the door.

"She's in our class?" The somber guy didn't move. "I'm Mark."

Mark said, "So am I." This didn't impress the kid. "Have a seat."

He ignored the invitation. "You probably heard about what happened. Which is why I might not make it to class today."

"I didn't hear anything about you."

"You will. It's all over campus. There was an incident. Last night." He was staring past Mark, out the window, over the pond, and deep into the rocky hills of the reservation land. "My car was stolen."

Mark said, "On campus?"

"Yeah. Well, nearby. Two guys from not around here, but they come around a lot, selling—they deal. Drugs, I guess. That's what I'm hearing anyway."

Mark said, "So they've been caught?"

"No, but we have witnesses." He sounded like someone who'd already talked to his father and his father's lawyer.

"Listen, you don't owe me any details. I'm just glad you weren't hurt. Let's talk about what this means for you in the workshop."

"There's not much to tell." He unzipped his parka halfway. "Me and a buddy wanted to go snowshoeing in the Breakheart hills while there was still snow, but there wasn't much. But anyway, I'd said I'd give a few other guys a ride out there, and those two black guys showed up with them, but for some reason the other kids decided they weren't in the mood, so those two black guys said they'd go with us for the hell of it. There was a big mix-up about what to do next, and I guess they ended up stealing the Audi."

Mark sincerely hoped this kid was a good skier because his story was going downhill really fast. "So you won't be in class today?"

He narrowed his gaze. It was the first time he seemed to be genuinely thinking before he spoke. "Probably not. Probably never again." He looked directly at Mark. "I am so fucked. Sorry."

"Is there some way I could be of use?"

"I doubt it," he said. "Thanks, anyway. I gotta go Skype with my parents again."

Mark said, "Send me an email when you feel up to it. We can meet to talk about your status in the class."

He zipped up his jacket, but it was too late. All the air had already gone out of him. "I can do that," he said, though it was obvious that neither Mark believed him.

2.

An ominous little eyelet of black water glistened in the middle of the pond, forcing Mark to follow the longer, circuitous path to class. He resented the detour. His bag was not especially heavy. He had his packet of the monosyllabic stories for today's workshops, the printed copies of the Professor's comments to hand out at the end of class, and fifteen copies of Technical Exercise 2, the hit-and-run story that would be due on Monday. But this Wednesday afternoon, he also carried Paul, and the other Mark, and those soggy bran flakes he should not have flushed down the drain, and Trump, and the Saab's rusty struts and axles. He carried them all the way up and into the Arts Building until the door of the Stanhope Forbes Seminar Room swung shut behind him, when he was unburdened, unbothered, unmindful of anything beyond the twelve faces turned toward him.

The room was silent, and Mark didn't say anything as he emptied out his bag. He did a quick recount. Only twelve, at last. Anton looked sheepishly pleased to have a seat at the table, and Mark knew that the other Mark would never be back to claim it. The Professor had not yet turned up. He often arrived in the middle of a class. Sometimes, if he'd done a round of radio interviews or a TV appearance, Mark couldn't rouse him for a couple of days. The Professor actually had a productive life as a writer. But his being late to class today and every Wednesday for the next few weeks of the semester was unrelated to his literary ambitions.

The Professor could not tolerate the first ten minutes of the Wednesday classes. He objected to Mark's habit of interviewing the students about their general impressions of the stories before beginning the workshops. The Professor thought this promoted generalization and encouraged the students to talk too much, which inevitably turned each five-minute workshop for a Technical Exercise into a seven- or ten-minute affair, which meant that the class work that could otherwise be completed on Wednesday reliably spilled over into the following Monday.

And those were the very reasons Mark refused to relent. Who didn't speak in generalizations about even the greatest novels, the most profound stories? *I loved that book. I didn't get the ending. It's really well written, but it was slow-going.* Why should students be expected to squelch that impulse? Of course, after that, there was more to say about each story—which often made it impossible to say all of it in five minutes.

Mark stood up. "Thanks for turning up again. We have three things on the docket. I want to do a quick review of any questions about the grammar and syntax material from last class. And then we'll start the workshops—they're our priority. We only have five or ten minutes for each story. When you are writing longer stories, we'll give them more time. For now, we'll talk fast. And we won't get to all of the stories today. But we have an open day on Monday, so everyone will get a full complement of comments."

"No pun intended." This was the small guy with the little ponytail. "Complement, compliment."

Willa said, "Why is that a pun, Max?"

Mark said, "It's wasn't quite."

Max tightened the elastic around his ponytail and said, "Well, it's a compliment that she knows my name."

Mark said, "Can you return the compliment?"

Max said, "Virginia?"

A young woman with almond eyes, a white headband, and two long braids said, "I'm Virginia."

Mark said, "I'm Mark, and I'm even worse at names than Max is, so let's try to say our names again today when we speak. We also want to preserve ten minutes near the end of class for the next story assignment. But I want to begin with your impressions of the stories you read for today."

"Good—oh, my name is Rashid." Her headscarf was emerald green.

Mark said, "Good?"

"Good. Not great. Mine included. Most of our stories didn't feel complete."

"Totally. Julio here." He was sporting a severe new crew cut, and the small patch of shiny black bristles made him seem massive, but because he never took off his parka, it was hard to tell if his bigness owed more to dumbbells or doughnuts. "Most of the stories were sort of abstract."

Mark said, "Intentionally so?"

Julio shrugged.

"No, not mine anyway. I'm Penelope."

Mark said, "Penelope?" He recovered quickly enough to add, "Why do you say the abstract quality wasn't intentional?" Her name was at odds with her appearance. She had short dark hair and bangs, and a broad, flat face with tiny features, like a pug. If he had to guess her ethnic roots—and he didn't have to, but he did—Mark would have wavered between Asian and Andean.

"I think a lot of us didn't make it clear who the people were, or why they were in a room together. And there were a lot of pronouns—so it was hard sorting out which he or she was doing what." Penelope raised her hands, as if fending off criticism. "I'm sorry, but in three or four of the stories, I couldn't even tell if the woman was dead or alive."

"That's not abstraction. That's a problem." The Professor had arrived. "I've met a lot of people, but I've never met anyone whose parents were so stupid or so forgetful that they didn't give their children names. Name your characters. Give them roles. In a few of these stories, we meet a nurse or a fry cook and—Presto!—we not only have real and memorable people, but a location, and a specific relationship between the man and the woman. Names, roles, location."

Leo said, "We're having a big name day."

Mark said, "Before you take out the story packets, I want to hear any and all questions or confusions you might have about the grammar we re-viewed last time. What matters most is that you feel confident about clauses and how to coordinate them."

All twelve heads were tipped forward, gazes aimed at the table. Mark wasn't sure if this was an aversion to syntax or to the Professor.

Three seconds elapsed before the Professor shouted, "Great. Everyone knows everything about syntax. Take out your packets."

"The order is irrelevant, just for the record." Mark wanted to restore goodwill before the workshops got going. He sat and said, "The stories are alphabetically arranged by first name."

Anton stiffened in his chair and then looked up, terrified.

Mark said, "Anton's story was not in the packet, but I have copies I'll pass out for everyone to read for Monday. We'll start with Charles." The whole class was still tense, so Mark slowly reviewed the rules for the ritual. The writer silently takes notes. Don't ask the writer questions or use her or his name—just refer to The Writer. Use the text to anchor your observations and confusions.

"And time is limited, so don't repeat what's already been said." The Professor could not contain his impatience. "You can second a question or en-dorse a comment, if you must, but leave it at that. Most important, bear in mind that the highest praise is serious criticism. It's of no use to a writer to be told you like something, or that it's good. That's what grandparents are for. Elevate your language. Endorse what you admire. Question what you don't understand. Correct what is clearly wrong."

"And we'll look for opportunities in the literal text—ideas or sugges-tions that are present and intriguing but not yet developed." Mark looked up for the first time in a while. All eyes were cast down on the text of Charles's story. And though Mark hadn't heard anyone enter with the Professor, in three of the six sunny windows on the southwestern wall sat a tall woman with braids, a small guy with wiry hair, and someone who was a ringer for Max. He hazarded a glance at the windows on the opposite wall, and he spotted a woman with short, greasy hair and a cowboy hat slung behind her head.

Mark concentrated on the twelve at the table. He managed to lead them through the stories by Charles, Dorothy, and Isaac in less than half an hour. He didn't pause. He flipped to the next stapled page and said, "Jane wrote a story. She titled it, 'Last Swim.' What should we say about it?"

"I endorse the title." This was Anton, who had endorsed one obvious element of each story so far, and then retreated into a protective hunch over his packet.

The Professor said, "Where is this woman, Anton?"

Anton bent so far forward that his spine audibly cracked. "A hospital? Or maybe a spa?"

Willa said, "I thought she was a lifeguard."

"A lifeguard? I thought the man was a guard—but a Nazi or something." This was Rashid. She looked around to see if she was alone in her interpretation, and she clearly saw the nods of agreement Mark saw. "Didn't she jump out the window?"

Isaac said, "She died? I thought she swam away."

Jane's head was bowed, but from ten feet away Mark could feel the red-hotness of the shame reflected from her face.

Mark said, "Does anyone have a confident sense of the writer's intention?"

The Professor said, "Name, role, location. Establish these in the first few lines of your story. And don't withhold narrative facts. My sense is that this writer wanted the identities of the man and the woman to be mysterious. But I don't want to get to the end of a story and find out—Oh! She's his mother! Oh! He's not a real shrink—he's a Nazi! I could have known that from the start. Don't withhold facts to create mystery. That's manipulation, and readers will sense it. The real mysteries of life are not withheld facts. The real mysteries are simple and persistent questions. *Why doesn't she love me? How could he say that?*"

Mark was desperately scanning the text of Jane's story for some laudable detail. "The monosyllabic diction is absolutely credible here." He paused, and Jane did look his way. Her freckles were coming clear as her embarrassment faded. But five of the six window ledges behind her were now occupied. Only the one directly behind Jane was empty. "And the sentences are terrific," Mark added, "so well made that I think we were all pulled along by the beautiful prose without ever getting anchored in a precise location or situation."

The Professor said, "And someone might want to sell this writer a Tab button."

"It's true," Mark said, "more paragraphs would help here. More paragraphs and shorter paragraphs will reliably serve your story. They are invaluable as a way to identify a new speaker or actor, of course. But paragraphing also highlights sequence for the reader. With each paragraph break, we sense time passing. Paragraphs infuse your fiction with the logic of time." He could feel the Professor preparing one final, all-out attack on the incomprehensible mess Jane had submitted, so Mark said, "Julio wrote a story," and flipped to the next page of the packet. After that, he led them through Leo's entertaining account of a female clerk who opened a revealing computer file—a Microsoft window—and skipped right past the other Mark's story, silencing any speculation about his absence by simply stating, "Mark is not here, and we won't talk about him behind his back," which left time for the story by Max. His story divided the class, as it did Mark and the Professor. Half the class thought Max had written a story about an elderly woman who freed a caged bird in a pet store and opened the window to let it escape. The other half—including Mark—read it as a kind of fable about an ill woman whose son would not help her kill herself. The debate delighted Max, and it delighted the Professor to call Max out—"You are not here, Max."—every time he so much as smiled or nodded during the controversy.

By then, nine of the window ledges were occupied. Mark didn't let himself dwell on that situation. He stood up. "For Monday, our order of events is Penelope, Rashid, Virginia, and Willa."

"What about Anton? Why did you leave him out?" This was Jane. Her tone made it clear she wanted some revenge for her miserable workshop. "He *is* in the class, isn't he?"

"I can save us some time," Anton said. "No names—check. No roles—check. No location—check. No paragraphs—check. Good workshop, guys. Thanks."

"Oh, Anton, you won't get off that easy." Mark stood up and passed around copies of Anton's story.

Before the pile was halfway around the table, the Professor said, "You're going to want to take notes." He was standing, staring down at the top sheet of the pile of assignments Mark had prepared, but he didn't pass around the printed copies of Technical Exercise 2. He claimed that the act of writing more immediately engaged the students' imaginations, that by taking notes they received the scenario as writers, not readers. Of course, it was Mark who would receive four or five emails asking for clarification later in the week.

"Here we go," said the Professor. "The challenge is to write a two-part story."

Scenario

Part I.

There are two people, a driver and a passenger, in a car moving along a dark road. It is very late at night or very early in the morning. The two people know each other rather well. They might be friends, blood relatives, romantic partners, or work colleagues.

The car hits something, and both people realize that the car hit a human being and that the victim is dead.

The driver slows or stops the car.

The passenger persuades the driver not to get out of the car and to drive away from the scene of the accident.

Part II.

Part II begins at least a week after the accident, but several months may have passed since that night. Let the reader know how much time has passed.

The two people are together. Maybe they are still in a relationship, or maybe they are not. You have to establish where they are and why they are there.

Something happens—this might be as apparently insignificant as a gesture, a sound, or a spoken phrase, or it might be a more dramatic event—that reminds both of them of the accident.

Write the story. Assume your readers know nothing about the characters or their situation when you begin.

Limits
1. No more than 250 words.
2. Part I must be at least 125 words long. Along with your name, please include the word counts for both parts I and II on your story.
3. Use first-person narration. Both parts of the story must be told by the same character, either the driver or the passenger.
4. The narrator must use present-tense verbs to tell both parts of the story.

Here, the Professor paused. "Questions?"

The room exploded, but Max yelled the loudest. "Each part is 250 words or the whole story?"

Mark said, "The whole story."

Max persisted. "But the assignment is more than 250 words."

The Professor said, "The boy can count."

Rashid asked for quiet, which worked. "Does the person have to die—and do both people in the car know for sure the person is dead before they leave?"

Someone else asked if both parts had to be told by the same narrator.

"Yes, and Yes," the Professor said.

Mark said, "And bear in mind that hitting a person by accident is not a crime. Leaving the scene—that is the moment that turns an accident into a crime. So this is a story about persuasion."

"Which is to say, this is the illumination of a relationship," the Professor added. "Why is one person susceptible to the suggestion or insistence of the other person?"

This silenced everyone for a few seconds.

"All present-tense verbs?" This was Penelope. She'd somehow managed to scrunch up her face and make it even smaller than normal. "Who is the narrator talking to?"

"Exactly," said the Professor.

Isaac wanted to know if Part I could be more than 125 words.

"Yes," said the Professor.

Then Isaac wanted to know if the characters had to be caught or punished in Part II.

"No," said the Professor, unhelpful as ever.

"Whether they get caught or not is a narrative fact," Mark said. "That's not the real mystery. You have to account for at least a week in this story. Whenever you encompass a large amount of time, you are writing about consequences. The mystery you have to address is what happens to the relationship and to these two people over time. Does their crime bind them to each other? Does it force them apart? That is the real story in Part II. That's what the action should illuminate for readers."

"And one more thing," the Professor said.

"Here it comes," Penelope said. "Use only words that begin with the letter *Z*?"

"Use only words with twelve consonants," said Rashid.

The Professor said, "Part I must be a single, perfect, perfectly grammatical sentence—that is, the sentence must adhere to the conventions of standard English grammar and syntax. And forget about semicolons. They are still banned."

All twelve of the heads at the table turned to the front of the room, and all twelve mouths opened. "One sentence?"

The Professor said, "You didn't have any questions about syntax when you were asked earlier. Here is your chance to demonstrate your mastery of English grammar."

Someone said, "A 125-word sentence?"

Mark scanned the room. The sun was setting outside. There was a silhouetted figure in each of the twelve windows.

The Professor said, "A perfect, conventional English sentence. Mind your choice of conjunctions."

Mark said, "Due by 8 a.m. on Monday in my email box. On your way out of class, I'll hand you the responses to your first story, Technical Exercise 1."

The Professor said, "And what did he say about extensions?"

Mark said, "No. Never. None."

The Professor said, "Now, collect your comments and go away."

And they did—almost. As they grabbed the Professor's responses to their stories, each one of the students glanced down and stopped somewhere shy of the door. Mark heard whispering from within the traffic jam.

He typed all his comments? Is all of this about just my story? Jesus, there's two pages here. Did he put footnotes on yours, too? He wrote more than I did. Whoa, this is serious.

Mark saw Willa turn his way, but as he stood to talk to her, he realized that she was simply trying to pull her cowboy hat up over her coat collar. And then he waved to acknowledge Rashid's "Thanks!" but it was actually directed at Julio, who was holding the door for her. Before the rest of the crowd cleared, the Professor was gone, and though Mark expected Anton to hang around for a minute to celebrate the good luck of getting into the class, he had also slipped away.

He smiled at the empty ledges of the twelve dark windows and said, "Dismissed."

3.

Mark was halfway around the pond when he heard someone shouting his name. He stopped and turned, looking for a familiar face among the students streaming by both ways, and then gave up and headed toward the garage until he heard his name again, and again, and again. Little Red Riding Hood appeared at his side. He recognized her freckled face and her voice, but he could not come up with a name.

"Are you going back to Hum Hall?" she asked, and she never paused again. "I can walk with you, but I can't go up to your office right now because I have my Russian Novels class back in that other Forbes room and she's bound to give us a quiz because at least half the class obviously watched the movie instead of reading *Anna Karenina*, and now we're all going to pay for that, but what I wanted to say is what if the man in my story is not just one or the other but both—he's got, like, an official role as the woman's guard or keeper or something, and he knows she needs to be guarded, you know, protected from herself, but he also cares for her, wants to help her, maybe do something he can't do in his official role, or maybe even shouldn't, but does?"

Mark could recall every word of her story, and almost every word that had been said about it during her harsh workshop, but he could not remember her name. Her getup didn't help. She was short, so the red-wool hood hid most of her face. He stopped at the front door of Hum Hall. "You're asking a really profound question. The thing is, on Monday, we're going to talk about this very challenge—how to balance disclosure and suggestion."

She nodded, but that last bit had clearly flown right over her hood.

Mark tried again. "I think what people were trying to say in your workshop is that they don't want to be surprised and feel like fools."

"No twist endings," she said.

"Yes—and no. We do want to know something more, something new by the story's end. But we want to feel it is an illumination of what we were shown earlier but did not clearly or fully understand when we saw it. Don't aim for shock alone. We want to aim for the shock of recognition."

"So, it can work?" She pushed back her hood.

Alice? Katy? Olivia? Mark gave up. "It can work."

"So I don't have to entirely change my story? I promise you, he's not a Nazi."

"That's a relief," Mark said. The Common was almost empty. "Don't be late for the Russians."

"Oh, thanks for that." She pulled up her hood. "And thanks for this. Thanks for everything." As she sped away, she yelled, "Thanks again!"

Mark hurried upstairs, stuck the key in his office door, and only then realized he had no reason to be in Hum Hall. He would have walked away, but from inside, someone yelled, "It's open. Come in."

Karen Cole swiveled around in her plastic chair and waved. "I can leave if you're meeting with students."

"Hello, Karen." She was wearing jeans and a white angora sweater, her uniform. "Aren't your classes Tuesday/Thursday?"

She shoved a few folders to the center of her little white desk. "Meeting."

"Don't move. I'm meeting no one." Mark dropped his bag on his desk. "How's the semester so far?"

"The poetry class is fine. The translation seminar is a joke. I have eight students who can barely read Italian, and I have one of those so-what-you're-saying-is idiots who turn up every time I try to teach translation. You know, he keeps retranslating everything I translate into a complete mistranslation of whatever it was we're working on. Sorry, I have to take this." She zipped out of the office with her phone at her ear.

Mark pulled out the packet of stories and found Red Riding Hood's. Jane, for god's sake. Jane. Jane. Jane. Still, he knew it wouldn't stick. He pulled a pen from his bag, crossed out her typed name, and printed *Jane Austen*. That he might remember.

And then Anton walked in, panting. "I'm so out of shape. And I used to run cross-country. Is she in our class?"

Mark said, "Who?"

Anton said, "With the fuzzy white sweater."

"Her name is Karen Cole," Mark said. "She's teaches Italian."

"Am I in our class?" Anton heaved out a couple of big breaths, and then patted the front of his jeans, slapped at his chest, and finally located his phone in a back pocket. "When I checked StudentServe after class, it said I was registered. See?" He held the screen toward Mark, as if it were a passport.

Mark nodded at the illegible lines of blurry type. But what he saw clearly was Anton's uncertainty, as if he suspected that his credentials might not get him across the border.

"I read all the typed notes on my first story," Anton said, and then he paused. "I got a lot of notes," he added. "So I guess I thought I should double-check with you, not just about being officially registered but about what you really think about me being in there."

Mark didn't say anything. Anton wasn't really talking to Mark. He was talking to himself. This Anton bore little resemblance to the poised, confident Anton that Mark had invented for his hit-and-run story. This Anton actually reminded Mark of Jane, both of them confounded by the gap between what they meant when they wrote their stories and what those stories meant to everyone who read them. Anton had found himself at an uncomfortable distance from his familiar idea of himself.

"Are you not saying anything because I should've said I wondered what you think about *I* being in there? Or is it *my* being in there? See, this is exactly what happens to me like ten times a day now, thanks to you," Anton said, and he quickly added, "and I don't mean that in the good way that happens while we're all together in class and you feel like you're supposed to be confused, or not so sure of your opinions or—I think you called them *reflexes*, which, by the way, I totally agree is what I have all the time instead of real thoughts—genuine ideas, as you like to say—so I guess my point is that I'm afraid it's only going to get worse with that new Technical Exercise you gave us today, forcing us to use so much grammar for that one long sentence."

Mark pointed to the chair beside his desk.

Anton said, "Are you saying sit down and maybe shut up for a minute?"

"It's worth a shot," Mark said.

Anton sat down.

Mark sat down and said, "Hello, Anton."

Anton said, "Hello, Mark."

Mark nodded. "This is starting to resemble a normal conversation. What brings you here today?"

Anton narrowed his gaze. Maybe he was suppressing a smile, maybe he was biting his tongue. "So, now I'm not sure what I want to say."

"Okay," Mark said.

Anton leaned forward in the chair, clearly expecting Mark to say something more. His interest slowly faded into a wry smile. "I know it'll just make you happy if I say I'm nervous or confused about anything. Right?"

Mark nodded. "Sounds like me."

"See, it's like I can hear your answer to everything I'm about to say."

Mark didn't say anything.

Anton ducked his head and coughed, or maybe he giggled. He was smiling broadly when he said, "All I can think about now is that long sentence I have to write."

"I was thinking about that, too," Mark said. It was true. "Do you remember what you said when you first got here? All that ten-times-a-day business and reflexive thinking?"

Anton winced. "Can we maybe agree just to forget I said all that?"

"If you counted, I think you'd see that sentence was almost 125 words long—and perfectly grammatical."

"I should've been taking notes," Anton said. He stood up. "I'm only leaving because I have an appointment. But you don't mind if I just come by again without an appointment or anything?"

"I'm already looking forward to the next time."

"I bet," Anton said, and waved on his way out, and then he turned from the hall and said, "It was really grammatical? What I said?"

Mark said, "Perfectly," and then Anton nodded and disappeared.

Although there was nothing else for him to do in his office, Mark felt obliged to wait for Karen to return—they'd known each other for years, and hadn't seen each other since the blowup last semester—so he checked his phone.

Paul was there.

Mark sat down. He had four emails, many texts, and a video. He immediately put his phone to sleep, tucked it into his bag, and decided to spend the night in Cambridge with Paul.

The door swung open. "I thought you'd be gone." Karen seemed more disappointed than surprised.

"I'll get out of your way."

"It's a union meeting. In here. I'm on the steering committee, helping to organize before the vote in May. I hope you don't mind." She pulled a pair of red-plastic reading glasses from a desk drawer.

Mark said, "It's your office as much as it is mine," though when Karen sat at her little desk, Mark did feel she ought to be taking dictation or lighting his cigar.

"I don't want to leave things where we left them last semester, Mark. I know you honestly feel strongly about the tenure system. I respect that. But it does seem wrong to oppose the union because white-collar workers aren't laborers, or simply—"

"I've never spoken publicly against the adjuncts unionizing. And the white-collar business—that came from some dean or vice president, not from me." He had noticed that there were usually ten or fifteen full-time union job openings on the Hellman food-service and groundskeeping staffs, but he didn't suggest Karen or her colleagues submit applications. "The thing is, Karen, unlike you and almost everyone in America, I think what really matters here is what happens in the classroom. I don't think it will survive unless it's protected. It's fragile. It's available nowhere else in the world. And I don't want a union organizer at the table when decisions about the classroom get made. It's that simple."

Karen held her glasses in front of her face, as she would a magnifying glass, or a rifle sight. "But doesn't it also matter that half the people who teach here can't afford to pay 85 percent of the premium for the college's gold-plated insurance plan so they go without any health insurance? While you get 85 percent paid for? It's a simple inequity."

"Unalike does not necessarily mean inequitable," Mark said, but that sounded more didactic than conciliatory. "Anyway, whoever is right here, it can't be a good thing that you and I are left feeling like opponents. I regret letting that happen. I haven't got a surplus of friends."

"And I don't think you're a partisan for the administration—I know you're not—and I really regret most of what I said the last time we had this argument."

Mark noted her *most*. "I hope we don't end up feeling like opponents when the vote carries. I do believe it will carry. There will be a union." He headed to the door.

"Hey, I didn't even ask about your classes," Karen said. "Are they okay?"

"You know me. I'm a sap. I just love time in the classroom." He waved and closed the door as he left, and he didn't turn around. He didn't go back and remind Karen he had a full-time, tenured position, with full benefits, a full-size desk and chair, and was teaching only one class this semester.

4.

Mark had to make three trips from the parking spot he found a block away from Paul's place with the groceries he'd bought, and after he'd shoved all but two bags into the elevator, the door closed and he was stuck waiting for whoever wanted to come down, who would also be stuck if they objected to standing on orange peppers, canned tomatoes, and the other makings for two or three weeks' worth of dinners. The walking back and forth, the heavy bags, even the wait for the elevator that was starting to seem sort of excessive—all of it was adding to his anticipatory pleasure, elongating the period of delayed gratification he'd planned since he first saw and didn't read the many messages from Paul on his phone.

They spent a lot of time apart, but this time, Paul had almost slipped away. It happened occasionally—how or why, Mark didn't understand. There was never a single precipitating event or an emotional upheaval that occasioned the near loss of him. From the moment Mark first laid eyes on Paul—which immediately provoked an absolutely mutual and absolutely urgent need to get every other body part involved in the introductions—knowing Paul was loving Paul was being with Paul. Distance, disagreements, discouragement, even apparent disasters didn't alter the degree or intensity of the desire, the need to be together. It wasn't variable because it wasn't a quantity or a quality.

But then there would be that breath Mark couldn't catch, the beat that ought to follow on the last one but didn't come when the muscles of his heart inexplicably froze. For how long this time? Time enough to feel the vast hollowed-out cavity of his chest, the futility of himself.

The elevator door slid open. The grocery bags were gone. Dennis Blake said, "Be brutal. How do I look?" He was wearing a tux.

"Spectacular." It was true. "Wherever you're going, you're gonna ruin the night for a lot of other guys," Mark said. This was true, too. Every man who put on a tux believed he looked like Dennis, and evidence to the contrary wouldn't be welcome news.

"Paul has this code." Dennis punched the code into the elevator keypad to keep the door open. "I put the groceries near your front door."

Mark had memorized and forgotten the code a dozen times. "How did you know they were mine?"

"Ipswich Seafood canvas bags. Wild guess. I really look all right? You'd go home with me?"

"I'd let you buy me a drink," Mark said. If Dennis's head got any bigger, he'd never get out of the elevator.

"I wish you'd told me you were here this weekend. We're going to the Vineyard tomorrow for some unknown reason." He tugged at his sleeve to consult his platinum dinner plate of a watch. "By now, food is being served and Diana is not speaking to me. Ten-Eleven. The code."

Although it was still locked in place, Dennis held the door while Mark tossed the other bags into the elevator. To reassure him, Mark said, "Ten-Eleven."

"Easy to remember," Dennis said. "It's my birthday."

After he shoved the last two grocery bags onto the kitchen counter, Mark set himself up at Paul's desk in the bedroom, emptied out his bag, and immediately printed the emails and texts from Paul. He didn't read them. He did read and respond to four student emails, an urgent request for an RSVP to an English Department meeting at noon on Monday, and he saved a few invitations to readings and dinners that were far enough in the future that Paul might want to attend.

At midnight, he packed the last of a dozen orange peppers stuffed with mushrooms and ground turkey, swimming in a stew of San Marzano tomatoes and caramelized onions, into Paul's freezer. The two quarts of Empire applesauce he'd made were already hardening in the way back. And the vat of brown rice was cool enough to go into the refrigerator alongside three garlicky pork tenderloins he could feed off for a week or two, with the addition of lemon and capers, which Mark considered a green vegetable.

He poured the dregs from the coffee pot into his old McClintock College travel mug and went up to the roof for a cigarette. He sat in Dennis's chair and balanced his mug on the arm of the other chair, his chair. The snow cover had melted up there and everywhere down below except the edges of the paths through the Cambridge Common. A thin spread of clouds had slipped in above, a curtain drawn over the waning moon and its attendant stars, those radiant hieroglyphics people had been reading for centuries. The night air was deep and dark.

Paul had found and preserved the old travel mug Mark had lost for months somewhere in the Saab. Paul was there. This was Paul's place.

Paul wasn't going anywhere. It was Mark who was slipping away. His love for Paul had not waned or wavered. But Mark had never been able to disentangle his passions and his ambitions, and with Paul so far away and so long gone, Mark was letting so much of himself go that he wasn't sure he could ever collect it all again, get a handle on who he was. He felt he was living in a little avalanche of undoneness and postponements and disinclinations—the chairmanship of the English Department he was doing his best to dodge; the NEPCAJE report he did not want to write; the friends and colleagues he didn't want to see; the week of spring break he didn't want to spend in Italy with that report not written; the ten days of the winter break he hadn't spent skiing in Utah with Paul and five of their friends so he could roam around his little house in Ipswich and occasionally stop at the threshold of his office to stare accusingly at the stack of sixty-five double-spaced pages of the novel he had abandoned. Unable to make himself write anything, Mark had called his loyal and long-suffering editor to complain that only one of the books he'd written was still yielding any royalties, so what was the point anyway? His editor said one perennial seller was one more than most writers could claim, and followed up with an email outlining several plausible op-ed topics to boost sales again, along with a list of periodicals likely to publish the pieces. Mark responded by devoting the remainder of his winter break to revising and refining the spring syllabus and Technical Exercises for the creative-writing class.

You could call this fear of success or fear of failure. You could say that Mark was embarrassed by his ambitions or unequal to them. He had diagnosed himself a dozen times but had not come up with a cure, except in the classroom. There, the Professor provided a potent remedy. The Professor's unapologetic, often punishing ambitions for the course and for the students' stories freed Mark to cultivate a relationship with each student, to identify this one's peculiar deficiencies and that one's idiosyncratic skills, to devote himself entirely to making room for them, even when it required shutting the Professor up or shoving him out of the way.

Dennis appeared on the roof in his tux. "Don't say a word." He eased down into Mark's chair, picked up the travel cup and took a swig. "Coffee. That'll help." He took a second, longer pull and then offered it to Mark.

"The back hall smells great," Dennis said. "What did you make?"

"Pork for me. Peppers for Paul."

"His favorite." Dennis didn't know it, but he knew more about Mark and Paul than most of their oldest friends and all of their many colleagues at work. The weeknight meals Mark made every Sunday, the four times of day they phoned each other, Paul's meticulous accounting and investment strategies on both their behalves, and the apparently astonishing fact that they still slept in the same bed.

Mark said, "I made a lot of applesauce if you want some."

"Frozen?"

Mark nodded.

Dennis said, "I'll wait till Paul gets back. But look what I have for us." He pulled a black box out of his breast pocket, about the size of a coaster. "From Russia. Genuine Sobranies." He flipped up the top and pulled out two black cigarettes with gold filter tips. He lit one, handed it to Mark, and lit another for himself.

Mark took a couple of long drags. The tobacco was dark, loamy. "It tastes like a peat bog. It's fantastic."

"It does feel dirty," Dennis said.

"Illicit," Mark said.

Dennis said, "I'd quit for good if I could just smoke a couple of these every day." He handed the box to Mark.

Mark said, "They're really called Black Russians."

"They're yours, comrade. I got a carton from some realtor who's trying to sell me something."

Mark held up the box. "Do you know what this means?" Reverse-printed in Cyrillic on a white background were two words: КУРЕНИЕ УБИВАЕТ.

"Smoking kills." Dennis extended his arm and held his cigarette at an admiring distance. "Here's hoping." He took two more drags, and then he followed Mark down to the landing, where they went their separate ways.

Back inside, Mark put on Paul's bathrobe and lay on the bed. The subject line of the first and every subsequent email from Paul was "Ten Percent." Perfect.

Paul had resurrected that subject line from years earlier, when Mark was still at McClintock College, writing a book to beef up his tenure box. Mark's plan to spend a few weekends doing interviews and research in San Francisco had turned into biweekly trips to the West Coast that fall. And months later, three weeks into his winter break, alone in a tiny little room on the top floor of a brothel with a disco bar near Union Square, he was still not done. Paul reassured him, loyally read every page Mark wrote, every day assuring Mark that he would cross the finish line. But that was precisely what had unnerved Mark. He knew he would stick it out, write the book, and get tenure, even as he felt Paul slipping away.

Paul repeatedly said he wasn't going anywhere.

Mark repeatedly said that wasn't exactly the point.

And then Mark wrote Paul an insane and insanely long email, a nearly verbatim transcription of his thoughts about Paul, about tenure, about writing, about how many times the same drag queen had knocked on his door and yelled *Room service!* He sent it with the subject line "One Percent." And then he wrote a follow-up email to explain that the previous email represented 1 percent of the thoughts and ideas he had hatched and not expressed to Paul in the last hour or so.

Paul answered immediately, under the subject line "Ten Percent." Mark had preserved the email, transferring it to every device he ever owned, the only item in his *Paul* file.

You have at least ten times more thoughts per minute than I do, so this will seem pathetically brief. I am here. I checked—I tapped my head, and I definitely felt my hand on my head. And if I am here, I am there, because I am the Paul you make possible.

In the fullness of time, we were always together.

5.

After reading through Paul's latest texts and emails a few times, Mark managed to paste together a reasonable version of the story on the European front. The administrative processing center and refugee camp on Lesbos where Paul had hoped to set up operations was overrun and overwhelmed. He'd quickly determined that the time required to coordinate the ongoing efforts with new staff brought in by the Paean Project would be counterproductive. Plus, many of the smugglers were now dumping their human cargo in smaller ports and bays where there was no police presence to interfere with their lucrative business. So Paul and two doctors had hired a fisherman to ferry them around the Aegean for two weeks to identify a couple of coastal towns that could be cajoled or bribed to serve as satellite bases where refugees could be transported for medical treatment beyond the emergency aid available at most of the established camps.

Paul promised to write something every day and hoped he would land somewhere with cell service at least once or twice during the adventure to send it all along. The video was a twelve-second view of a forty-foot trawler and two shirtless guys with ponytails mugging for the camera. The crew? The doctors? Paul's baggage handlers?

When he woke up on Thursday morning, Mark sent off the first of the daily One Percent emails he had resolved to write every morning till Paul returned. He also forwarded the video to Paul's great friend, Sharon, the nurse who had Paul's car, and asked if she was free for dinner next week. This was progress. He was getting hold of himself, and he hadn't even had a coffee yet. Mark was on the way back. He read an email from the dean organizing the NEPCAJE meeting at Amherst, one week from Saturday, which threatened to derail his progress. Two of the four people scheduled to join Mark on the featured panel had pulled out. Did Mark have a colleague he could bring along?

Mark's immediate response was envy for the two dropouts who wouldn't be wasting a Saturday in Amherst. His next move was to pour a cup of coffee and wander around Paul's living room, trying to gin up a plausible excuse for skipping the event. But the last time Mark skipped an NEPCAJE meeting, this same dean had assigned him the task of writing up the literature review. And the only prospect grimmer than a round trip to Western Massachusetts was a round trip with any colleague who had nothing better to do on a weekend. It was a simple Yes or No question. But Mark was stumped.

He could invite the Professor.

This thought required a refill on the coffee, and with that in hand, Mark parked himself at Paul's desk and reread the dean's email. Yes or No?

What would the Professor do?

For starters, the Professor would give a lecture on the power of conjunctions, and while Mark imagined that delightful interlude, he also imagined that the Professor would surely beg off or simply ignore the request. Mark had no intention of actually composing an email to the Professor. But he responded to the dean with a perfectly Professorial Yes but/and/so No. Yes, he would pass on the request to an eminently qualified colleague, *but* he could not guarantee the Professor would be willing or able to attend, *and* Mark wasn't even certain the Professor would respond, *so* if the dean did not hear from Mark again by tomorrow morning, No, he could not count on the Professor.

The dean responded immediately. *Fingers crossed!*

And then an email from Sharon popped up, agreeing to dinner next Wednesday, and with another cup of coffee, Mark had regained his resolve. He was back on track. It was not even ten thirty, so there was no need to readjust his plan for the next four days. He would work on the NEPCAJE literature review today and Friday, and then drive to Ipswich and spend two days working on that abandoned novel.

There was a pile of dishes to deal with first. And after half a Black Russian on the roof, Mark thought the cooking smells from the night before were hanging around longer than normal. He switched the exhaust fan on. It sounded sort of feeble. He lit the other half of the Black Russian, took a drag, and watched his exhaled smoke loiter around above the stove, amused by the fan but not drawn in. It was probably forty years old. He ducked his head under the hood, and that did it. Replacing it would be easier than scraping off enough of the accumulated grease so he could unglue the ancient, clotted filter. Which led him to the exhaust fan in the bathroom, which led to five trips to two different hardware stores over the next four days, a touch-up paint job that turned into two new coats on the entire bathroom ceiling, and so much horsepower that you could vacuum-clean the carpet in the living room by just turning both new fans on high.

6.

Mark was ten minutes late to the department meeting on Monday. He sat near the back, at the top of the vertiginously raked concert hall. The room had five hundred seats, and about thirty were occupied. A mini Mount Rushmore of suited and polished vice presidents and deans had been installed behind a table on the stage, under the watchful eye of one of the college's many lawyers, a youngish woman in pearls standing at a podium, for some reason. They would be delivering the same news to each of the college's departmental faculties over the next few days—to full-timers only. They were laying down the law about communication with the Other Side during the run-up to the vote on the unionization of adjunct faculty.

Mark recognized the backs of many heads and the familiar features of the many active Twitter, Instagram, and Facebook feeds. The Professor was nowhere to be seen. Althea Morgan was marooned in the middle of the very front row. Maybe she felt it was her duty as chair, but she did look like the only person paying attention until she stood up to take off her coat, turned briefly, and gave everyone the finger, aiming it back at the stage. The lawyer picked up a little device and illuminated an overhead projection of Faculty & Staff Protocols on the screen behind the panel. Mark estimated that he'd transgressed at least four of the enumerated boundaries during his conversation with Karen Cole.

The air in the room was getting warm and a little squalid, and after he devoted almost twenty minutes to an inspection of the HVAC vents and fans overhead, he saw the venerable Norman Chester, emeritus, wobbling up toward the exit and rushed to his assistance.

Chester gladly took hold of Mark's arm, and while he paused to catch his breath before heading out the door, he pulled Mark in close and said, "What a collection of fuck buckets."

Outside, Mark offered to walk him to his car, but Chester pointed to a new black SUV parked in the fire lane ten feet away.

"Think they'll get their union?" he asked.

"I do," Mark said. "Frankly, I think the administration will be relieved. They don't want to waste their time worrying about what goes on in classrooms."

"They've got meetings to attend. Can I give you a lift?"

"I'm teaching soon, just up the hill," Mark said.

"I hear those workshops of yours are quite the draw," Chester said. "I don't know if this sounds barmy, but I envy you."

"Here's what's barmy," Mark said. "I like the teaching so much I envy me."

Chester tumbled into his car, but he wasn't having much luck closing the door, so Mark waited for him to get himself realigned and then sealed him in and waved goodbye. When he reached the top of the hill and started to cross the Common, Chester screeched to a stop beside him, blasted his horn, and lowered his window. "That lawyer on stage? I did the math. The college pays her more every year than it pays the entire first-year comp faculty—all adjuncts. I added it all up." He waved and drove away.

7.

Mark was five minutes early to class, and his entrance didn't interrupt the lively conversation underway.

"Maybe that analogy makes sense if you're white," Dorothy said. She was a terrific writer, and she looked like the black Buddha, though better coiffed, with her hair extensions and beads. Although she hadn't spoken much in class, she seemed to be at the center of this discussion.

"I wouldn't know what makes sense to white people," Julio said indignantly. Stroking his shiny black flattop, he added, "*Nací en Quito, hermana.*"

"I'm sorry, but you still can't compare the history of American slavery to anything," Dorothy said unapologetically.

"Well, the Jews were enslaved," Max said. His ponytail had migrated up his head into a little yellow man bun.

"Were they sold?" This was either Dorothy again or Rashid.

"They were exterminated," said Max. "Which is sort of harder to live with."

"Those two guys who stole his car aren't dead, and they're not at Auschwitz." Leo looked at Mark but didn't stop to fill him in. "How did they become the victims all of a sudden?"

"I heard Mark started that rumor so he wouldn't get expelled." Willa looked up and smiled. "Not you, Mark, the other Mark."

Someone said, "If he got kicked out, why is he still living on campus?"

Leo said, "Mark said—this Mark, I mean, our Mark said we're not supposed to talk about the other Mark behind his back." The entire class slowly turned to Leo. Evidently, it was up to him to sanction any further discussion. For a few seconds, he was paralyzed by the attention, as if his bulky ivory hand-knit sweater were a full-body cast. Finally, he shrugged, staring right at Mark. "Right?" He threw up his hands—but he had only one hand. The right arm of his sweater ended somewhere near the elbow.

Mark nodded in answer to Leo's question. But how had he not noticed Leo's missing hand? How would Leo handle the reams of paper that would be passed around the table this semester? Did he type his own stories? Were his classmates unaware, uninterested, or unnerved? Was it odd, or alarming, or a relief for Leo that no one at the table had asked him to tell that story?

Willa tipped her cowboy hat off her head. "Anyway, I heard those two guys didn't steal the car at all."

"They're black. Ergo, on this campus, they stole the car," Dorothy said.

Mark looked at his watch. One minute to three.

"But they aren't black, are they?" Jane paused. "Not exactly, anyway. They're from Fall River." This was met with stunned silence, so Jane and her amazing freckles ventured deeper into the controversy. "Or New Bedford? Somewhere on the South Shore. I think they're from Brazil."

Anton said, "Probably Cape Verde."

Someone said, "Cape Verde is in Africa."

"No, it's not," Anton said. "It's an island."

Mark said, "Penelope wrote a story." He paused just long enough for phones to disappear, packets to be unfurled, and the other-Mark mystery to dissipate. "She titled it 'End in Sight.' What needs to be said about it?"

And they were off.

The Professor never showed up, which occurred to Mark too late to curb the enthusiasm for the open-window stories by Penelope, Rashid, Virginia, and Willa. Each of their workshops ran on for almost fifteen minutes. And when Dorothy pointed out that almost all of them had killed off their central characters, several people jumped in with speculation about why that was so, and Mark looked up for the first time in a while and saw that eleven of the window ledges were occupied by familiar silhouettes, and while he registered their ghostly presence, the remainder of the class time was almost diverted into a free-for-all discussion about the morality of imagining and orchestrating someone's death.

To quell the crowd, Mark stood up and said, "I want to talk about your responsibility as writers—not only how you handle the fate of your characters, but the language you assign them, as well. But for right now, Anton wrote a story. He hasn't yet titled it."

Anton said, "Let's be honest, it's not good."

Mark said, "You're not here, Anton."

Anton said, "I wish I wasn't."

Mark said, "Weren't."

Leo said, "Weren't? I wish I weren't. Really?"

Mark said, "Really."

Rashid said, "It's the subjunctive." She didn't seem convinced. "Isn't it?"

"It is," Mark said, "which I am officially adding to the growing list of Future Topics. For now, suffice it to say, yesterday, Anton wasn't in this room, and today he wishes he weren't. But he is, and I want to know what you have to say about his story."

No one spoke for a few seconds. Dorothy said, "Well, *again, over, because, already, into, windy, open, wooden, outside,* and a few others aren't monosyllables. But the writer's idea that the air outside is poisonous—I totally endorse that."

Anton picked up his pen and underlined something.

Mark saw that the window behind him was occupied. Twelve, at last.

Julio said, "Is that why the guy yelled at her about the heat?"

"Yeah, yeah, of course," Dorothy said. "And the dead things outside. The whole setting—I endorse that, too. It's got some problems with the syntax, but it's original. This was the only really dystopic story."

Anton looked up beseechingly.

Mark stood up and said, "It's a great word, and I want to make sure everyone knows the form Dorothy used." On the blackboard, he wrote *Utopia* and *Dystopia,* and after he explained the distinction, a couple of the faces at the table did not look entirely enlightened, so he added *Functional* and *Dysfunctional* beneath the first pair. That seemed to work, so beneath those, he wrote *Myopia* and *Myopic*, to make sure Anton and everyone else understood that the altered ending of *dystopic* was a familiar convention.

Time was up. "I know it's four thirty, but don't move. I want to thank you all for getting the work done again. I received all twelve new stories. On time. Top-notch adult behavior. I have a new packet of stories for each of you."

Rashid said, "The dreaded long sentence."

"If mine is a sentence," said Leo.

Mark said, "Starting Wednesday, I'm going to ask that you pass the writer your annotated reading copy of her or his story at the end of each workshop. Your editorial notes don't have to be formal, or elaborate. A question mark next to an underlined passage is often as useful as a long comment. But do aim for legible. This will also make it possible for us to spend less time talking about minor issues that are best handled on the page, leaving more time for—for the art of it."

Willa said, "Did you say *the art of it*?"

Mark said, "I did."

Max said, "Don't look a gift horse in the mouth."

Dorothy said, "Don't miss a chance to use a cliché."

Willa said, "I so wish I was an English major."

Rashid said, "*Were*. I wish I were."

"Oh, Mark, how could you?" This was Max again. "You've put us all in the subjunctive mood."

Mark tapped his watch. "And I owe you four minutes. Now, go away."

When the classroom cleared, Mark expected the Professor to turn up with an explanation for his absence, and this persisted as he erased the blackboard and shoved all the chairs back into place around the table, packed up his bag and headed to the garage. It haunted him all the way to Paul's place, through dinner, and two Black Russians on the roof.

On Tuesday morning, Mark did write another One Percent email to Paul, but the NEPCAJE books proved as repellant as ever, and his resolve to work on the novel would have required a trip to Ipswich to retrieve the manuscript, so he turned on the new fans to admire his handiwork, and they sucked up and disposed of the rest of the day. For lunch and dinner, he had coffee, so he was wide awake when the Professor finally delivered his comments on Technical Exercise 2 late Tuesday night.

Mark smoked a Black Russian to brace himself for the Professor's latest assault.

Mark Sternum / Technical Exercise 2.

The prose work here is genuinely impressive, and you handle the distended syntax of the long first sentence with apparent ease. (I am well aware that it was not easily done. You might be surprised to know that I really am a fan of your writing, not only in these short stories—which I really think you might consider submitting to one of the better journals for publication, should you be willing to go public—but of your nonfiction work, as well.)

I am not entirely confident that readers who don't identify Anton as a student simply by mention of his name will be immediately drawn in to the fullness of the story (I was—and I found the breakneck speed at which that happened really rewarding). You might want to find some way to at least establish his youth (if not his status as your student) right from the start. That's a minor consideration in a very successful and sophisticated piece of work.

I do think the seduction—or the suggestion of same—ought to be rethought. Why not give the narrator agency, have him caress or stroke Anton? Isn't that why the narrator climbs into the pickup? Isn't he hoping for something more than a ride to the beach? Or, perhaps what you mean to suggest is that Anton initiates the attempt at intimacy? Do you want readers to see that Anton has misinterpreted his teacher's intentions, that the narrator (notably, he never does acquire a name over the course of the story) has simply been an alert, engaged, and even affectionate presence in the young man's unhappy life but unaware of the effect he has had on his stu-

Technical Exercise 2

(Mark Sternum / 250 words: Part I 183/Part II 67)

At midnight, my phone rings, and Anton giddily announces he's outside in a pickup, so I grab my parka, but he won't lower his window, forcing me into the passenger seat, and he floors it, squeals past a stop sign, and soon we're sailing down icy curves to the beach, and maybe because he's wearing sunglasses, I announce I can't joyride with my student, and he says he's not any more, his parents cut him off and he got a job plowing snow, but don't worry, he whispers, rubbing my thigh, he'll be back next semester, and then a reflective yellow vest catches the headlights, and the pickup clips the jogger, slams her into the pavement, blood spilling from her misshapen skull as Anton skids to a stop, hyperventilating, and when I open my door, he confesses he's fucked up and carrying, pulls a pipe from his pocket as proof and defeatedly folds the sunglasses into their protective case, so I glance at the woman—the corpse—and the dark, dark road ahead and order Anton to pull a U-turn and follow my directions.

Anton disappears, as instructed. The case goes unsolved for a blessed month, and then a horn honks during a snowstorm. Anton's pickup is sporting a plow attachment.

He rolls down his window. "After you convinced me to drive away." His eyes are bloodshot.

"What?"

"It's a dependent clause. Unfinished." Anton slams down the plow blade, revealing his pickup's mangled front end.

A neighbor's porch light flips on.

Comment [m1]: Is the absence of a title an affectation? Is it meant to be suggestive? (It is not.) For the record, all 12 student stories are titled.

Comment [m2]: The opening pace is terrific. And though I get the idea, I'm not confident we understand why the narrator feels compelled to get in the truck. Or is the implication that he is more eager to get in than he is willing to admit?

Comment [m3]: Awkward: sailing down

Comment [m4]: Really? At midnight?

Comment [m5]: Invented verb. Intentional?

Comment [m6]: Syntax not quite working as intended ("any more" is esp. imprecise).

Comment [m7]: What prompts a whisper here? (Why lower his voice right then?)

Comment [m8]: Hmm. Are you sure it's not the narrator who rubs Anton's thigh—perhaps allegedly to comfort him?

Comment [m9]: This is a superb sequence.

Comment [m10]: Odd word choice, given Anton's behavior earlier, taking the lead in all their interactions. (Again, rethink the seductive thigh business, where we might see how Anton has been subtly manipulated all along by the narrator.)

Comment [m11]: It's an efficient word, but it is a novel coinage. Intentional?

Comment [m12]: Beautiful detail.

Comment [m13]: I know you're out of words, but with a few judicious cuts, you could make room to get his name (or, at least, "he") into the last clause. Something very potently instructor-ish about "Anton follows my directions."

Comment [m14]: Not sure about this word.

Comment [m15]: Is this the most elegant phrase available? (Genuine question.)

Comment [m16]: I think he could choose a stronger, more suggestive verb here.

Comment [m17]: This is a risk. I mean, I get the aim, but are you sure this is precisely what he says? Maybe more credible without "It's a"?

Comment [m18]: Try moving this to the end of this paragraph, after the blade bangs down.

dent? (That's absolutely plausible, but readers will need to see some evidence of that in the literal text.)

Of course, these and all of my other questions and concerns are matters of nuance and fine-tuning, as I hope is evident from my line-by-line notes. Your prose here is so confident, and your respect (you would say "love") for the Technical Limits is so total that I am really happy to devote my time to your little stories, week after week, and I am hoping you will be able to set aside some time to return the favor.

Presently, I am at work on a couple of op-eds for the *New York Times* or maybe the *National Geographic* in support of THAT BOOK (your phrase—my emphatic caps), which does inexplicably prove perennially popular. It might please you to know that I also have a novel underway, though I suspect it will be a few weeks, at least, before I am ready to submit those pages to your scrutiny. If you can see your way clear to give the op-eds a good going-over, I will have a rough draft of the first to you in a week's time, or so. As always, my extensive responses to the new student stories follow.

THREE

Technical Exercise 3.

(Mark Sternum / 498 words)

The Professor typically slowed as he drove past yard sales only to marvel at the junk people considered valuable. But it was June, sunny at last, and instead of inchoate student stories on the passenger seat, he had a flat of tomato plants. Plus, one table in the yard was piled high with books. As he pulled over, two young guys loaded a mountain bike missing its front wheel into an old black Cadillac that looked like a hearse.

The books were handsome, hardbound, and of no interest—college textbooks, an encyclopedia of American music, biographies of Papa This, Joe That, and other apparently admirable and dead bluegrass pioneers. There was also a silver harmonica someone thought was worth $40, an electronic keyboard, and a banjo in a black case lined with red satin.

More interesting were two stout women—lesbians?—wrestling with an old Boy Scout tent, both glancing beseechingly at the big, bearish man on a lawn chair inside the garage.

From across the patchy brown lawn, a blonde yelled, "Richard!" She was at a picnic table, her hand on a cash box. She headed toward the garage.

Richard stepped out into the light and winced. He was wearing a too-small Oberlin sweatshirt, holding a bent bicycle wheel.

As she approached, the blonde—Richard's wife, surely—said, "That bike is finally gone," and grabbed the bent wheel. "You have to let it go." As she passed the Professor on her way to the tent, she said, "How about fifteen for the encyclopedia?"

Richard sidled up to the Professor and whispered, "Do me a favor?" His breath smelled boozy. "Buy the harmonica."

The Professor said, "I don't play."

The two guys who'd bought the bike were back, pounding on the un-plugged keyboard, as if by sheer force they could bring it back to life.

Richard slid two twenties under the harmonica and whispered, "Follow me." As he walked toward the picnic table, he paused and lowered the lid on the banjo.

By then, the tent was open. Richard's wife said it was priced at fifty, but the lesbians could have it for forty.

One of the lesbians found a sleeping bag inside the tent. "It's warm," she said. "Sort of creepy."

Richard's wife said, "Twenty-five?" She sounded desperate or irate when she said, "It's all going for a music scholarship."

The lesbians hightailed it to their car.

The young guys seemed to be eyeing the two twenties, so the Professor followed Richard to the picnic table, handed him the cash and the harmonica. "I don't want this."

Richard closed his eyes, pressed the harmonica to his lips for a few seconds, and then pocketed it. He yelled, "Sold!" and waved the twenties for his wife to see. His eyes were teary. "So awfully quiet around here."

The Professor decided Richard was drunk. To mollify him, and to amuse himself, he said, "You drive a hard bargain," and headed for his car, hoping his young seedlings weren't dead.

* * *

1.

Mark knew his yard-sale story was not a success, but he'd devoted almost four hours to it on Wednesday morning—well, three hours of real writing and several trips up to the roof to finish off his supply of Black Russians and watch purple snow clouds huff in from the south. Despite his doubts about the quality, doing the work of embracing and trying to love the assigned limits, inventing characters, and writing and rejecting and revising made him mindful of the work all of the students would do after they got this assignment in class today, none of which the Professor would deign to do.

Mark reread the Professor's complimentary response to his hit-and-run story one more time, surprised and more than a little embarrassed by how it pleased him. Of course, it was bait, but Mark had swallowed it, and now he was on the hook to devote his time to those op-eds, which would yield more TV time for the Professor, more royalties for *that book* he'd been milking for almost a decade, and for Mark? More time away from the festering wound of a novel abandoned on his desk in Ipswich. This morning, though, he had just enough time to print out copies of the assignment the Professor would not distribute to the students, shower, and get to campus for office hours before class.

Mark was ten minutes late. Anton was sitting cross-legged on the floor in Hum Hall, his back against Mark's office door, next to a pile of something red and puffy.

"I have a question." Anton scrambled to his feet, dragging the puffy red mess with him.

Mark unlocked the door and said, "Tell me that's a parka."

"It's red," Anton said, dragging the coat as if it were a screaming child. "My mother claims it's called a car coat. I'd rather have the car." He looked around for someplace to dispose of the garment.

Mark said, "It's supposed to snow later."

Anton said, "It's red and shiny, and I really don't want to talk about it."

He tossed the coat onto the floor and sat in the alumni chair. He stared out the windows, as if he might be regretting his decision to come inside. He was wearing his uniform yellow V-neck, but no scarf.

Mark slipped his little blue parka onto the back of his chair. "What's your question?"

"So, I love this class," Anton said.

Mark said, "That makes me happy. That's my aim."

Anton smiled so broadly that he strained the muscles in his neck. "I knew you'd say something like that."

Mark said, "It's true."

"I know," Anton said, and then he ducked his head and tugged down one sleeve of his sweater to wipe his eyes. After a few seconds, he whispered, "What I said—that's true, too." He wiped his sleeve across his eyes again. "I didn't expect to start crying like that. Sorry." He kept his head bowed. "Maybe I just like loving something again."

"Versus, say, the coat," Mark said, hoping to lighten the mood.

"Exactly." Anton finally raised his head and smiled. "So, I wanted to say I know sometimes I look tired or like I'm not paying attention, but I'm never tired in class, Mark. That's the truth. I'm not drawing or doodling or anything like that. I try to write down almost everything you say, and even Rashid, and Max, and Dorothy constantly say stuff I totally understand when I'm in there but I know I won't remember afterwards, or even if I do, I won't get it by then, not the way it makes perfect sense in class." Anton slid forward in the chair and braced his hands on his thighs.

Mark nodded. Anton seemed to be heading somewhere he wasn't sure he wanted to go in this conversation, and Mark didn't want to urge him on or stop him. "It is a really good group."

"So, I just wanted to let you know they think it's temporary," Anton said, sliding back in the chair and grabbing both armrests, "and after a couple more times this new chemo drug shouldn't be screwing up my memory like the last one. And since my hair isn't falling out like they promised, maybe they're right."

"Here's hoping," Mark said, narrowing his gaze, tacitly accepting the pretense that he knew about Anton's illness.

"This new drug works out for our class because it's late on Mondays when I go to the clinic, after class," Anton said. "Infusions, they're called. That leaves me Tuesday for Netflix and juice, basically, and I feel fine by Wednesday when we have class again, and I just wanted you to know it's just some kind of leukemia, which sometimes can be cured."

The shock of Anton's revelation was also an illumination. The diagnosis threw new light onto his shaved head, the after-class appointments, and his status as a fifth-year senior—notable but not extraordinary details that suddenly cohered into something much more suggestive. "I hate that you're sick, Anton."

Anton nodded. "I knew you would."

Mark waited until he was fairly confident he wouldn't cry when he spoke. "And I'm happy—really happy to know there are people taking care of you, doing everything that can be done to get you back to—to being yourself."

"More people than I need, really." Right on cue, Anton's phone buzzed. He slapped his pants pocket and silenced it. "One thing about being Cape Verdean is everybody within a hundred square miles is your aunt or cousin."

A knock at the door startled them both. Mark signaled to Anton to stay put and stuck his head out far enough to see Leo kneeling with his backpack between his legs, unzipping it with his only hand. He had something else strapped over one shoulder. A few feet away, Dorothy and the curling-team guy with the Maple Leafs jersey both waved.

Leo said, "I could come back at two thirty."

Mark said, "It's a date. Knock if the door is closed."

From down the hall, the Maple Leaf yelled, "I'm in sort of a rush."

Mark said, "I'm not. Give us five minutes," and closed the door.

Anton said, "Is it okay to ask why my story was first in the packet this week?"

New topic; so noted. Mark said, "Alphabetical order by first name."

"Okay." Anton stood up. "I was afraid it was another bomb." He turned to leave.

Mark said, "Sit for one more minute, Anton."

He did.

Mark said, "You know I will always be interested in how you're faring, and you don't owe me any more in the way of updates or information. Your call. Whatever happens week to week with your health, however, we can make it work for you in the class. That's my call."

Anton said, "Thanks, Mark."

Mark said, "You're welcome, Anton. And one more thing—and."

Anton said, "And?"

Mark said, "And, and, and, and, and, and, and—"

Anton groaned. "I knew it. I knew it. The hit-and-run story—I screwed up that 125-word sentence. I should've thrown in a *but*."

"Or an *or, because, yet, so*—anything. The good news is that your long sentence is actually perfect grammatically, but I did sort of feel I was in an echo chamber by the thirteenth or fourteenth *and*."

Anton said, "Could you give me a list of words that are conjunctions?"

Mark was about to pull a pen and pad from his bag, but stood up instead. "I was just thinking. If someone ever invents Google Search, I bet he'll make a fortune."

"Okay, okay." Anton stood up. Before he left, he turned. "But the story—not just the sentence, the whole story—that was pretty good?"

"We'll find out in workshop when your readers respond."

"Perfect grammar, though. Perfect?"

Mark nodded.

Anton nodded and slipped out into the hall.

Dorothy came in, sat down, and glanced disapprovingly at Anton's shiny red car coat on the floor. "Isaac asked me to tell you he had to leave, but he might stop by later."

Isaac? Isaac? Mark could not put a face to the name. More notably, the beads and extensions were gone from Dorothy's braids, and she was wearing an oddly old-fashioned navy blazer and skirt, and black pumps. Mark was still standing behind Dorothy. He didn't say anything. He felt momentarily like a kid who'd been called before the principal.

Dorothy briefly looked back at him, and then turned away. "Hello, Mark," she said, tucking her skirt underneath her thighs. "How are you today?"

"Well, I'm fine, Dorothy. How kind of you to ask," he said, a little too aptly imitating her cheerfully professional tone. He sat at his desk and aimed for a more casual tone. "What's up?"

"Well, partly I wanted to just say how much I'm enjoying the class. I especially love the Technical Exercises. They're sort of infectious. I find myself thinking about them all the time. Then, I read what everyone else wrote and wonder why I didn't think of that."

Mark said, "You're doing really great work."

"It's not easy, which is hard to explain to anybody not in the class. I mean, 250 words sounds like nothing."

"To someone who isn't a writer."

Dorothy nodded. "Like my father." She kicked off her shoes. "Was that rude?"

Mark wasn't sure if she was talking about kicking off her shoes or kicking her father to the curb. "They look painful."

"So's this." She peeled off the blazer and tossed it onto Anton's car coat. The office was starting to resemble a rummage sale. "I had an interview at a law firm in Boston this morning. My father's firm—well, he's a partner, and he thinks I ought to work for a year before starting law school."

"Law school where?"

"Stanford."

Mark said, "What a terrific place to land, Dorothy. Congratulations."

"Thanks. And feel free to say so to my father if you run into him at commencement." She smiled confidentially. "Harvard man."

Mark nodded. He didn't say, So am I, which Paul would say proved he was a Harvard man. Dorothy produced a revision of the first, monosyllabic Technical Exercise, which Mark read aloud and then discussed with her, annotating her new text with a few question marks—four choices for her to reconsider. She looked it over and hummed her approval. After she folded it in half, she looked down at her blazer, as if she were debating its fate. But, as it turned out, she had been debating her own.

"Here goes," she said, and after a long pause, she asked if he'd be willing to write a letter recommending her for a summer internship with a publishing house in the Bay Area. "They probably want someone younger, a sophomore or junior who might end up working there at some point," Dorothy said, "but it would be perfect for me, so I think it's worth applying. It's reading unsolicited manuscripts, and that would sort of be like our workshops, I thought, and maybe motivate me to keep writing."

"That alone is reason enough for me to write the letter," Mark said.

"I think you might know them," she said. "Plus, I just saw on their website that they publish Wendell Berry. You know who he is, right?"

Mark nodded. They were also the publishers of *that book*, on which the Professor had made a minor media career.

"Last semester, we read a lot of Wendell Berry essays in a course on land rights as civil rights. I didn't really know it then but I'm starting to think that might be the sort of work I want to do with a law degree."

Mark said, "Research and writing?"

Dorothy nodded and placed her bare feet on top of her pumps. She angled her feet this way and that. She was either debating whether to say something else about her ambitions, or she was wondering how she was going to jam her feet back into those shoes. "You know how in our class, you sometimes suddenly see yourself? Somebody is talking about your story, somebody you sort of know, and she calls you The Writer instead of calling you by name? Or maybe even more when it's someone you have your doubts about—Max or Leo is explaining some word or sentence you wrote to everyone else, deciding what it means, and you realize it's his property now? Yours and his?" She kicked her shoes back under the chair.

Mark heard a conversation outside his office door, but whoever was waiting out there had yet to knock. He said, "Maybe intellectual property law is in your future."

"Property, for sure. Something to do with property, which seems so simple but in the law is so—"

Mark said, "Complicated?"

"Honestly, I was trying not to say *fucked up*."

Not trying too hard. "Is it a paid internship?"

"No, but I can live with my mom and stepdad in Oakland for the summer."

Doubling her father's delight, no doubt—no gap year working at his firm, and a summer with the stepfather. "I'll happily write on your behalf, Dorothy." He knew the Professor might balk at writing a letter to his publisher on behalf of a student, but that didn't mean *that book* couldn't be flogged to someone else's advantage for a change.

Before she left with her shoes dangling from one hand, Dorothy had located her phone in a pocket of her blazer and emailed Mark her CV, a description of the internship, a copy of the application letter she'd written, and the name and email address of the woman to whom his letter had to be addressed—having determined in a matter of minutes her plan for the summer, the following year, and maybe the rest of her life.

Leo was alone in the hall, with his backpack slung over one shoulder, a camera with a telephoto lens slung over the other, and his phone in his hand. "Am I too late? I apologize. Isaac came by but says he'll talk to you after class."

Isaac? Isaac? Again, nothing.

Leo said, "I should've emailed to let you know I'd be late. I got hung up taking pictures down the hill. Sorry."

"We've got five minutes anyway," Mark said. "Sit." Leo didn't move, and Mark reflexively worried that Leo wasn't able to maneuver into the chair with all that equipment and only one hand. "Do you want me to hold something for you, Leo?"

Leo misunderstood this as a reprimand. "Oh, but I wasn't texting. I was just shutting it off." He untied a drawstring on the side of the backpack, slid his phone into a little pocket, and tied the string in a quick square knot. "It's this camera. It's borrowed and worth a fortune, so I'm sure I'm gonna do something stupid and regret it. Would it be okay to set it on that white kiddie desk by the window?"

Mark nodded at Karen Cole's ridiculous little adjunct office allotment.

"I'm doing a project. I was wondering—or—" Leo returned from the window and sat down. "Sorry. Did you want to talk first?" In size, shape, and coloring he was a standard-issue American college kid, but his eyes were so black they were luminous with reflected light.

Mark said, "I've been talking too much today. You go first."

"Thanks. It's about this project I don't understand yet. And my girlfriend says it's too obvious for the class. Not our class. I'm taking a documentary photography class. Anyway, I think she means I'm not being not artistic, not original enough. But I've been thinking about what you said, about not wanting to talk to us about our ideas but only about what's on the page—how when it's on the page, it starts to have possibilities? You said that, right?"

"It sounds like something I'd say," Mark said.

"So, for now, I'm not thinking too much. I did want to ask permission to stay after class and take pictures of our classroom."

"With everyone in the room?"

"No. Empty. I've been taking pictures of every room on campus where I've had a class during the last four years. Honestly, I don't know why."

Almost immediately, Mark's memory rolled out still shots of the many and various rooms on the Hellman campus that had been home to his classes over the years. "I don't know why this is so," Mark said, "but that's really suggestive. Somehow a little haunting."

"Right?" Leo stood up and retrieved his camera. He placed it on Mark's desk. "You want to see the two I just took? I have real film in here for printing, but you can look at the digital images." He knelt beside Mark's chair and positioned the tiny viewing window at a perfect angle for Mark. "I mean, they are obvious, but—"

"But they're not." Mark thought he recognized both rooms, but they seemed strangely severe and standardized. "Is this one the new theater?" Up close, Leo smelled like a Marlboro, or at least Mark hoped Leo was the smoky one.

"I had New Wave Films in that theater when I was a sophomore," Leo said. "First time I saw *Blow Up.*"

Mark didn't say, Antonioni.

Leo said, "Antonioni."

Mark nodded. "We should head to class. And you have my permission to stay after for as long as you need."

Leo pulled a square of paper from his back pocket and unfolded it. "If you don't mind signing, so I have official permission to go into other classrooms? It's about promising not to destroy college property, but I'm just taking pictures. I need a faculty sponsor. I won't hurt anything."

"I'm happy to vouch for you, Leo." Mark quickly read the form, or as much of it as anyone who wasn't a lawyer could bother to read. "Did you not want to ask your photography professor to sign this?"

"She can't. She's part-time, so they don't trust her, I guess."

Mark said, "Adjunct."

Leo said, "I might want to shoot our classroom again if we get a sunny day."

"Also fine."

Leo was packed up, with his equipment re-slung and his phone in hand before Mark found his coat on the back of his chair.

2.

Leo took the only empty seat at the far end of the table. Mark unpacked his bag. In the four minutes before the start of class, almost everyone was rating spring break destinations—Cabo, Cozumel, South Beach, and St. Croix were the popular favorites. The other-Mark stolen-car controversy had either been resolved or forgotten, or maybe it had only momentarily sunk below the surface of campus life, roiling away and ready to explode again at any moment.

With a couple of minutes yet to tick away, Mark pulled out the final registration sheet he'd printed from StudentServe. He was looking for Isaac, but before he found him, his gaze landed on a photo of Charles. Charles? For a panicky moment, Mark couldn't recall anything about Charles. The picture—taken when he was a freshman—showed a sullen, big-shouldered boy, with a smooth, long hank of hair carefully arranged to cover most of the left side of his face. No one at the table even vaguely resembled the photo. In truth, all twelve first-year photos of these seniors were so useless that they might have been supplied by the Witness Protection Program.

"Did Dorothy tell you I want to meet with you after class today?" This had to be Isaac, helpfully wearing his Maple Leafs jersey, as usual. He was nearest to Mark's left.

"I'll stay, and we can talk here. Will that work?"

Isaac nodded and texted something.

It was past three by the time Mark managed to identify Charles. He was two down from Isaac, and deep in private conversation with Rashid, who was wearing a canary-yellow headscarf today. Charles was a rotund guy in a pale blue button-down shirt, several sizes too small for him. He had red hair and an embarrassingly sparse crop of wispy red whiskers that he seemed to believe had cohered into a beard.

Mark said, "What did you make of the hit-and-run stories?"

As phones clicked off, and packets appeared, either Charles or Rashid whispered that they were trans and thought the other one knew that they had just started to transition. Mark looked at Isaac, who had ducked under the table to get his stuff and apparently heard nothing of his neighbors' conversation. Everyone else at the table seemed equally unaware or uninterested in the gender bulletin.

Anton said, "I thought the grammar was pretty good," shamelessly aiming for public praise.

"But in Part II—after they leave the scene of the accident?" Penelope brushed her bangs back while she paged through the packet. "Well, I marked most of them as incomplete."

"Pity parties," said Max, who had foregone his man bun today, his shiny blond hair falling neatly around the collar of his blousy white shirt, further complicating the gender-identity question. "Even mine," he added, "now that I see how much it follows the pattern."

"I agree," Dorothy said. "There's a lot of, like, oh, poor us, we killed some guy, and now we have to live with it."

Leo said, "Penelope's was the one I endorse. I mean, if your wife is giving birth, that's a reason to drive away."

Willa said, "Even if you just killed someone?"

Charles said, "How about Rashid's, with the driver being drunk? That's a reason not to dial 9-1-1."

"Virginia's is the only one—I think so, anyway—hers is the only story where the car gets damaged," said Dorothy. "I didn't think about that till I read hers, but it's—you know—"

"Physics," Mark said. "It does apply. Or it ought to. When I was reading the stories this week, I often felt I believed in the world the writer had invented more than the writer did. And on second reading, even though most of you handled the distended syntax of that first sentence well, I thought the logic of the narration was pretty weak, and a lot of the choices the couples made seemed adolescent, not adult." He sensed from the stiffening faces at the table that his tone was too sharp, tilting toward punitive. He decided to finish the sermon and then woo them back slowly. "The clauses work, by and large, in that long sentence, in a strict grammatical sense, but the narrative sequencing seemed haphazard to me because so often we're stuck in the mind of the narrator, where anything can happen, where no logic applies. The arena for your stories has to be the world. And in your literal texts, you have to give readers some signposts to highlight sequence and logic."

"Conjunctions," the Professor barked. It was his arrival that had altered the mood in the room, and he didn't seem displeased by the reaction he was getting. "Every word counts. The first Technical Exercise, that monosyllabic story, was not a game or a loosening-up exercise to make you feel good about yourselves. I don't want you to feel good. I want you to feel anxious and uncertain. I want you to be self-conscious about every choice you make, unnerved every time you have to choose the next word. With the monosyllables, you discovered you have the capacity to choose. Now, use it."

Someone said, "Or lose it," someone who hadn't registered the Professor's tone of voice.

"Thank you for that, a stellar example of words that were not chosen. And when that variety of language turns up in your narrative prose—as it too often does—it doesn't register as lived, as particular. It's automatic writing. You are all quick to point out clichés in each others' work, but unlike automatic writing, chosen clichés are useful and often illuminating. I mean, the first time I went to Paris, I wanted to see the Eiffel Tower. And I did. And I took a picture of it. A cliché, of course, and something that made me see precisely what I did not want to believe about myself—that I was not the singular, sophisticated adventurer I liked to think I was but one in a long line of tourists, indulging an impulse that marked me as not French, not cool, not who I thought I was, not the young man I wanted others to see. It's not always the original, unheard of, alarming detail that matters most, but the well-chosen one. Don't choose to surprise me. Choose to illuminate me. That's the power you have as writers. And with the power of choice comes the responsibility for wielding it."

The Professor was roaming around the room now, and Mark wasn't sure where he was headed.

"Someone died in each of the stories you wrote this week. A human being. You orchestrated the killing, and you plotted the escape of the perpetrators. That is on you. It's not enough to say it happens all the time. It's not enough simply to assert that the hateful and irresponsible action taken by your characters reflects the morals of those two people in the car, and then leave it at that. No more than it is enough to script your characters to spew hate speech or other stupidities and pretend you didn't write it, that you would never say such things when you clearly do—in fact, you did in many of the stories we're reviewing today. You required your characters to utter those vulgarities for you."

Mark thought it might be time to step back in, but the Professor was not done.

"You are the writer. Every time you write a story, I want you to know that you have access to every word in the language, as vulgar or inane as it might be. Never tolerate censorship. And don't cater to the tastes, or preferences, or PTSD of your reader. Choose any word, any action that serves your story. But know this—every choice you make redounds to you. I will always know you chose those words. You wanted me to read them. This week, each of you was responsible—not for murder, not as far as I know— but for illuminating for readers the consequences of reckless behavior. Instead, too often we get an accidental death, an immoral choice to flee the scene, and almost nothing by way of illumination. Figure this out. I have plenty of demands on my time. Why should I set aside those demands and read your story instead of reading about a hit-and-run in the newspaper? What makes your story necessary, new, unsettling? What about your story will alter the way an adult thinks or acts? Why else are you writing these things down?"

The room was eerily quiet. Every window ledge was unoccupied. Mark said, "Anton wrote a story."

Anton said, "And, and, and."

The Professor said, "You are not here, Anton."

And for a few silent seconds, it seemed that every other person at the table wished to be anywhere but right there. Willa timidly tipped off her cowboy hat and stuck it under her chair. Dorothy pried the staple out of the corner of her packet of today's stories. Jane and Penelope exchanged confounded glances across the table. The Professor repeatedly and rather too obviously glanced at Mark's watch, so Mark took it off his wrist and set it on the table.

"For the first five or six lines—" Rashid paused and pointed her pen at her copy of Anton's story. "Well, in the first three lines, actually, I like—I mean, I endorse the repeating *and* in the writer's long sentence. I felt it created a sense of carelessness, as if the driver wasn't paying attention—to what he was saying, where he was going, anything."

Leo said, "He sounded like a teenager, just babbling on for the sake of it. That makes sense of the crash."

"Until the crash," Rashid added. "After that, the *and*s started to seem—"

Max said, "More written than lived."

"I thought the narrator—do we ever learn his name?—I thought he was older, not a teenager," Dorothy said, still plying that staple. "In Part II, doesn't the couple live together?"

Anton was furiously taking notes, shadowed by Anton in the window directly behind him.

"I think they were at a motel in Part II, hiding out. The two double beds? They had been there before, before the story began—having an affair." Jane read a few lines of the story aloud to prove her point. "See, they go back to the motel after the accident and then are afraid to leave."

"I think Jane is right—on intent, I mean." Willa was rereading Anton's text as she spoke. "What doesn't make sense is that they must have been hiding out for a whole week. In Part I, we're led to believe the lovers have families. Do they really just ditch their lives?"

Isaac said, "It is a good reason for leaving the scene, though."

The Professor said, "A good reason?"

Isaac said, "A bad reason?"

Jane said, "Isaac means the affair is an explanation, if not an excuse for not wanting to be caught."

"Exactly," Isaac said.

"Couldn't have said it better himself," Max said.

Jane blushed, blotting out her freckles. Isaac didn't seem to register that the joke was on him.

A few of the windowsills were occupied, and the mood in the room had just started to tilt back toward normal when the Professor said, "Pass Anton your annotated drafts," as if giving orders to a bunch of recruits. "I'm giving each writer just five minutes today."

To counter that command, Mark said, "We are going to be brief in our comments today because on Monday, we're giving the floor to the writers for at least half an hour." This was pure improvisation. The Professor was a better drill sergeant and a better sermonizer than Mark, and because he had no interest whatsoever in the students' lives outside the classroom and rebuffed every attempt Mark made to share any facts about their health or families or personal struggles, the Professor was also a better and a more useful critic of their written work. It wasn't that the Professor could be objective, or even wanted to be. He was opinionated, provocative, and curious; a reliable, engaged, intelligent, and principled reader; a kind of North Star against which students could reliably gauge their progress on a singular journey. This was all a writer could ask for, and more than most of them would ever get again.

The Professor made writers of them. Over the course of a semester, each of them would write—and deliver on deadline, without fail—four very short stories, two full-length short stories, each one revised many times and often entirely rewritten, none with more than a few unintentional lapses in conventional syntax and grammar. It was an accomplishment most professional writers would envy.

The Professor did make writers of them, and it was impressive to witness this transformation. Mark couldn't make that happen. But he could do what the Professor would not. He could make room for them, the all of them, in the classroom—even if it wasn't always as elegant a place as the generous ledge below each of those twelve tall wavy-glassed windows in this beautiful room. Most of them had never written a decent story before they entered the classroom, and most of them might never write one after they left. Mark made room for them so they could see what was happening to them, so they could see themselves as writers, so that this moment in time would be forever fixed in their memories like one of Leo's snapshots, and they would know they had done something they did not know they could do, been someone they had never imagined they could be, and see that possibility in front of them for the rest of their lives. "So on Monday," he said, "we'll start the class with questions from each writer about what was said in workshop today, clear up any confusions, and then we'll look at strategies for revising, including how to make sense of contrary responses and suggestions from readers."

"Right now," the Professor said impatiently, "I want to get through this packet and preserve at least ten minutes to talk through the next Technical Exercise."

Mark counted eight figures in the windows. "Charles wrote a story," he said. And, sure enough, under the watchful eye of the Professor, each workshop was cut off at the five-minute limit, and when Willa was gathering up the annotated pages of her story, Mark checked his watch. There were ten minutes of class time left, and only the windowsill behind Isaac was unoccupied. Mark dug out the copies of Technical Exercise 3, but before he could remove the binder clip from the stack, the Professor said, "The challenge for Monday is to use suggestion artfully to reveal the truth that haunts a simple transaction."

Max said, "Scenario?"

The Professor nodded. "I hope your pens are poised." He read Mark's assignment almost word for word.

"There are two principal characters, a seller and a buyer. The setting is the yard outside the home of the seller. The occasion is a yard sale. The buyer and seller have never met before the sale. You can decide whether it was advertising or chance that led the buyer to the sale. Among the items for sale are three that must be identified in the story—a bicycle, some kind of musical instrument or music-playing machine, and a sleeping bag. All three of those items belonged to a child of the seller, and that child died recently—sometime during the last two years. And the buyer must pay for one of those three items. This is the story of a completed transaction. Assume your readers know nothing when you begin. There is no limit to the number of characters or items for sale."

Dorothy said, "Technical Limits?"

The Professor said, "No more than five hundred words. Use past-tense verbs to tell the story. Use third-person limited narration."

Several heads popped up. Mark said, "Remember, that's simpler than it sounds. The goal is to give readers omniscient access solely to the buyer. Readers can know the thoughts, impressions, and motives only of the buyer."

The Professor said, "By choosing to limit the omniscience to one character, you make her or him the central character. Your story becomes that character's story. All characters other than the one to whom we are limited can be understood only by what is apprehensible to the senses."

Mark said, "Not unlike the way you judge people in movies—by their appearance, facial expressions, actions, and speech. We can't know their thoughts."

The Professor said, "You will decide how strictly the narration is limited to the central character. Is every sentence of the story filtered through the mind of the central character—information about the time of day, or the physical setting and weather, for example—or do you want to establish an objective narrative voice to report some of those details? You can use the limited either way. What matters most is that readers are confident they know when to attribute an observation or impression to the character."

Anton, Isaac, Virginia, and maybe a few others had stopped writing. Mark said, "If you are confused or anxious about using third-person limited, do yourself a favor. Don't worry about making distinctions between objective and limited narration. In your mind, imagine the whole story is delivered from the point of view of the buyer. Everything readers see and hear is from that person's perspective."

The pens were moving again.

The Professor said, "The seller never directly refers to the child, the child's death, or the accident or illness that caused the child's death. The seller doesn't directly reveal anything about the loss or the emotions associated with the loss. However, by the story's end, readers should be aware of the seller's loss."

Max said, "What about the buyer? Does he know?"

Willa said, "Or she."

Someone said, "Or *they*."

The Professor ignored the pronoun controversy. "The buyer might understand as much as readers do by the end, or the buyer might remain unaware of the tragedy. That is your decision."

Mark said, "The real work of this story is to use suggestion, not hints and clues, and to use it artfully. The goal is to give readers the opportunity to appreciate the full significance of this sale indirectly, gradually. And I want you to know from the start, there is no formula or rule for achieving the perfect degree of suggestion."

"This isn't a science," the Professor added. "It's art. Ideally, when readers become aware that the seller has lost a child, they will recall memorable and unsettling details from earlier in the story that make perfect sense in retrospect."

Mark said, "That's why we call the end of a story a resolution. The implications and suggestions of the literal text are resolved, and the full meaning of the action we have witnessed comes into clear focus for us." Mark was about to repeat the deadline and delivery instructions, but the symphony of sighs stopped him. The room looked like a Victorian sweatshop, all twelve workers bent over their tatting or needlework.

When six or seven of the students sat back in their chairs, the Professor said, "Some of you will have read the famously short six-word story Hemingway wrote that bears on this assignment."

Mark turned and wrote on the board: *For sale: baby shoes, never worn.*

"I don't like that colon," Max said. "Unnecessary device."

"I question the syntax," said Dorothy.

"Isn't it a little odd to sell off your dead baby's stuff?" This was Rashid. "Why not give it away?"

"That's a profound question you're going to want to think about before you write," said Mark.

Anton asked, "Can our stories be that short?"

"Hemingway's tiny story is a model of efficiency," the Professor said. "It is not a model short story. Suggestive? Yes. But we have no central character, no dramatic arc, and nothing but the generic emotions we all associate with the death of an infant."

Mark was impressed—and a little appalled—by the Professor's surgical summary of the famous little story.

"On the other hand," the Professor continued, "you have a buyer—and that buyer is the central character whose story must alter or complicate our sense of ourselves. Illuminate your readers."

Mark was thinking of the yard sale story he had written—and how he hadn't really inscribed an arc for the character of the Professor.

The Professor said, "And mind the transaction."

"More on that on Monday," Mark said, putting on his watch.

"When it's too late to do anything about it," said Max.

"I'm happy to know that makes you nervous," said the Professor.

Mark was still thinking about his yard sale story, and now he worried that the oddball business with the harmonica and the seller's two $20 bills didn't really add up to a proper transaction. He put on his watch and saw that they were already ten minutes over time.

The Professor said, "Pick up your drafts of the hit-and-run story with my responses on the way out."

"Can you give us just one example of the difference between a hint and a suggestion?" This was Virginia, and her request was getting a lot of nods.

The Professor said, "A hint is singular. Suggestion is accretive."

Mark said, "An obituary notice—that's a hint. Someone saying 'I'm so sorry for your loss'—that's a hint. In one word or phrase, the death is made obvious. But a man who hasn't shaved for a couple of days, or an unkempt garden with lots of droopy flowers that haven't been dead-headed, or a woman dressed in black—by themselves, those might mean a man doesn't like to shave, or someone hasn't been doing yard chores lately, or that woman thinks she looks better in dark clothes. But as such details chosen by the writer accumulate—well, you get it, right? They become suggestive."

Leo said, "Can we use words like *deadheaded*?"

"You should," the Professor said. "Words that evoke death and dying or loss will echo suggestively."

"Eight a.m. on Monday morning in my mailbox, please," said Mark. "And thank you all for sticking around so long."

"Now, go away," said the Professor.

"Not you, Isaac," said Mark.

Isaac looked up accusingly, as if he'd been unfairly called out.

Although no one else in the mad rush to the door seemed to have heard him, Mark added, "You said you wanted to meet with me."

"Oh," Isaac said. "Yeah." Clearly, he had no idea what Mark was talking about. He loaded up his knapsack and rearranged a few items, stalling. Luckily, something he'd scribbled on his notebook tipped him off. "It's about those original short stories. I was reading the syllabus this morning and saw that we're starting them next week."

"We are," Mark said. Whether Isaac was more studious than he appeared or simply couldn't find a cereal box to read this morning, something nutritional had sunk in. "What's your question about the stories?"

"How would it be if I submitted drawings with my story? You know, like a graphic novel."

Mark didn't say, You mean a comic book? Instead he said, "Feel free to add drawings. I won't consider them part of the text, but if you want to include them, I won't object."

"No, see, the pictures are the story," Isaac said. "It's a new kind of writing."

Mark said, "Aren't pictures the old kind of writing—what people did before they learned to write?"

Isaac muttered, "There'd be some words."

"As you know, I'm a big fan of words," Mark said.

Isaac shoved his notebook into his bag.

"I don't want you to leave without this." He handed Isaac the annotated draft of his hit-and-run story. "And I'm happy to talk this through, Isaac, and explain why I won't treat illustrations as text," Mark said.

"Never mind," Isaac said. "I think I get the point."

Mark wasn't sure he did. But he didn't really know anything about Isaac yet beyond that Maple Leafs jersey he wore every day, so he went with that as his point of entry. "I don't want to forget to ask how the curling team is doing."

Isaac's mood visibly improved. "We're not a team, but we got club status—just today. That's why I couldn't hang around and wait for you in Hum Hall. I had to meet with some dean to sign the forms and everything."

"That's great. Well done. I ask because someone was talking to me about wanting to join the team." This was a risk, and not only because it was a lie. "He's got his own special broom."

"No," Isaac said, and then he looked genuinely confused. "I mean, sure, give him my email and tell him to be in touch. But we have an equipment budget now."

"No, no—that's the thing. He has his own broom he wants to use— only it's not really a broom. It's better."

Isaac seemed intrigued. "Better how?"

"It's got bristles like a broom, but it's also a vacuum cleaner."

Isaac said, "He wants to use a vacuum to curl with?"

"The suction makes all the difference, he says."

Isaac tilted back in his chair, apparently trying to get a new angle on this situation. "A vacuum cleaner," he said, just to make sure.

"Portable," Mark said, sensing that the absurdity was finally sinking in. "Battery-operated, so no cords. He says it's way better than the standard curling brooms."

"Like using pictures instead of words, you mean?" Finally, Isaac got it. "Very funny."

Mark said, "Not acceptable according to the rules of the sport?"

"Probably not," Isaac said. He tilted back toward the table. He stood up and smiled. "Here I was, trying to figure out a polite way to say no to your friend with the vacuum."

Mark nodded.

Isaac nodded, headed to the door and didn't look back, but when he was out in the hall, he yelled, "See you on Monday."

3.

It began to snow as Mark packed up his bag, big lazy flakes that smashed into the windows like hopeful, heedless moths. As he headed outside, he recognized the white headband and braids of the young woman sheltering under an eave of the Arts Building. Vanessa? Eleanor? The prospect of one more conversation was unappealing enough to make him back up and wait her out in the dark classroom, but as he hesitated, she turned and entered the building, her phone pressed to her cheek, and didn't acknowledge him. The snow made him mindful of Anton's coat crumpled up on his office floor, so he veered off toward Hum Hall.

It must have been after five because the front door was locked, and the windows of all but one of the departmental offices were dark. It was unclear what he might do with the puffy red coat if he retrieved it now. It was painfully clear that he'd have to climb up three flights of stairs to arrive at a decision that would probably leave him in possession of a winter coat Anton didn't want, would promise to take from Mark on Monday, and then leave in the classroom.

Mark was confident he knew Anton well enough to know he didn't want that coat. And there was a lot of snow in the air, and more on the way, and that NEPCAJE panel in Amherst on the horizon this weekend, so Mark made a beeline for the garage. The Saab wasn't happy to see him and balked the first few times Mark twisted the key in the ignition, but it finally relented. At the end of the exit ramp, a gust of wind greeted him. The snow was blinding now. He decided not to drive to Ipswich, which would make for a longer drive to Amherst on Saturday. Plus, he had several pork tenderloins at Paul's place. And he didn't need to stare at that abandoned novel on his desk to know what he wasn't doing with his spare time for the next few days.

Maybe it was kindness, maybe it was pity, maybe it was guilt—it was hard to name the principal currency of most transactions with students— but instead of heading directly to Cambridge, halfway down the hill Mark made a quick U-Turn toward Hum Hall and parked behind the back of the building, next to the only other car in the spaces reserved for office staff and administrators. He turned off the Saab, and as he braced himself for the climb up to his office to retrieve Anton's car coat, one of the young English Department assistant-somethings rushed out through the back door. Sybil? Cheryl?

She stopped and opened an umbrella. "Mark! Go home already. It's nasty out here."

"A student left something in my office."

"Shaved head? Yellow sweater?"

"Anton," Mark said.

"He came by about fifteen minutes ago to claim it."

"He did?" Even to Mark, the question sounded more accusatory than curious.

She raised her umbrella up an extra foot or so, to let Mark see the concern on her face. "He swore he had your permission to go into your office."

"Oh, he did. I'm just surprised he remembered where he left it. And you are a true champ. Now, go home."

"There's a bottle of wine waiting for me," she said, and rushed to her car and drove away.

Mark didn't. After fifteen minutes of jiggling the key in the ignition and whacking the dashboard—often a successful strategy with the Saab—he called Paul's automobile club. Twenty minutes later, he explained to the young guy with the tow truck that the battery was fine but nothing else seemed to be.

All the guy said for a while was, "Saabs." But after he'd poked around under the hood and plugged and unplugged the fuses under the steering wheel, he loosened up. This was his eleventh tow of the day, and with the weather, he figured he'd be out all night. He wasn't wearing a coat or gloves, but he complained bitterly about the cold. He was also evidently annoyed that the Saab had to be taken to Ipswich, though he did concede that Mark's mechanic, Ozzie, was an honest guy.

Mark mostly shrugged his way through the conversation, and texted Ozzie, who was never surprised to learn that the Saab was on its way to him.

As the tow truck operator hauled out the chains and cranked a couple of pulleys, knelt down on the wet hardtop and then slithered in under the car on his back to hook up the axle, Mark thought about this young man's life tonight, next year, twenty years on, and all of the books he'd recently read from experts opining on the worthlessness of a college education.

The tow truck driver said he could take Mark to Cambridge, but that would be an uncovered expense—maybe as much as $125, not including gas. Mark thanked him and ordered up an Uber. As he watched his Saab get dragged ignominiously off the field of battle once again, a white hatchback pulled into one of the empty parking spaces.

Karen Cole, his adjunct officemate, rolled down the front window. "Was that your Saab?"

Mark nodded. "Can't imagine why they stopped making them." He figured Karen was on campus for another union-organizing meeting, and he hoped his ride would arrive before the rest of the part-time faculty.

Karen said, "Get in."

"Oh, thanks," Mark said. "I'm actually headed home. I already called an Uber."

Karen said, "I'm your Uber."

Mark said, "No, I really did already call for a ride. Thanks, though."

"I'm your Uber driver, Mark. Harvard Square, right?" Karen blasted her horn. "I'm not getting out in this weather to open the door for you."

This was awkward. It reminded him of being served dinner or fitted for a pair of boots by a McClintock student three or four years after her graduation. Mark climbed into the back seat. "I'm staying at Paul's. Just above the Cambridge Common."

"I've got GPS," Karen said. "Do you mind NPR?"

As opposed to discussing the irony?

Karen turned up the volume on the radio. For the first time since November, the news out of Washington registered as a relief.

Karen wasn't a patient driver, but Mark's standards were low. She didn't hit anybody. That was good enough for him. When they were nearing his destination, he pulled out his phone and rated her a five-star driver on the Uber app. This was grade inflation, but Mark was an old hand at that pump.

As Karen pulled into a handicap space at the top of the Cambridge Common, she said, "I'm giving you five stars as a customer. I like the quiet ones."

Mark said, "I've already rated you."

"I know you gave me five stars," Karen said. "I checked. That's why I gave you five. Good night."

At Hellman, faculty members weren't allowed to read their student reviews until they'd given out final grades, which was fair but frustrating. Maybe Karen and her union would get that policy reversed.

While he was waiting for the elevator up to the fifth floor, Mark texted Paul's friend Sharon and asked to borrow back Paul's car. Sharon was delighted to surrender the car, as she was going out of town for ten days and would otherwise have to pay for off-street parking. Mark was delighted that Sharon wanted to skip their planned dinner for tonight and make the exchange on Friday morning after her shift at the hospital, as searching for on-street parking at night in Harvard Square after a snowstorm was simply a roundabout way of eventually paying for off-street parking.

4.

Mark got to the hospital early on Friday. Until recently, Sharon had worked at Harbor Hospice, a project she and three other women launched to provide end-of-life care to homeless people who would otherwise die on the street or in an emergency room. It was more than a decade since a newspaper story about their noble but ad hoc operation in an abandoned basement lab of one of the big university teaching hospitals had caught Mark's attention. He'd casually mentioned it to Paul, who took his brown-bag lunch for a walk the next day, found the basement, met Sharon, and spent the rest of that afternoon and most of the evening answering the one phone in the lab and greeting terminally ill people who had found their way to Harbor Hospice or been dumped in the doorway by someone who didn't know what else to do with them. Within six months, Paul was the chief operating officer, and a former convent was being converted into a proper home for Harbor House, and ten years later he finally persuaded two of the big medical schools in Boston to integrate the project into their better-outfitted and better-funded facilities. That's when Paul was recruited by the consortium of teaching hospitals to run the Paean Project, where Paul was hoping Sharon would soon join him, and where Mark was hoping Paul would spend more time in his Boston office.

Mark stood and watched from the counter of the intensive care unit desk as Sharon checked in with the last three of the critically ill people behind the twelve shower-curtained bays. She spoke so softly that the conversations were inaudible, but Mark could see her straightening out bed sheets, offering them cups of something, and pausing for a silent moment at the foot of each bed—meditating? praying?—before she made a few notes on the chart and then moved on. A doctor with a shiny swale of jet-black hair and a knee-length white coat was impatiently trailing Sharon, repeatedly looking at his wrist. He was leading a posse of short-coated students into each bay, where he picked up the chart from the foot of the bed, conducted a brief Q&A with his posse, and made a few cursory pronouncements about the patient's progress, often with his back to the person in the bed.

"Most of the doctors don't like to waste time talking to the patients," Sharon said after she'd found them an empty room with two chairs and a generous window ledge to eat lunch.

Mark said, "What's with his dye job?"

"Second marriage," Sharon said. "And now, instead of a watch, he wears one of those body monitors."

They exchanged a knowing nod. People often mistook them for siblings, and though neither of them could see a resemblance, their shared suspicion of well-groomed people and outdoor activities did lend them a distinctive rumpled pallor that might kindly be misconstrued as familial.

"I don't mind filling in here as needed for a few months, but I could never work full-time for doctors again."

Mark had seen doctors in action many times, and he'd watched rounds, but something about how little seemed to be required of the so-called expert had really impressed him today. "So the doctors are basically delivering summaries of what the nurses have been noticing and noting down, and—"

"Oh, my god." Sharon put down her sandwich and pried up one piece of bread. "What did you put in here?"

"Pork tenderloin, avocado, and havarti." Mark had brought bag lunches, as he always did for lunch with Sharon, not only because he admired her and could not imagine how to thank her for the work she did, and not only because lunch would otherwise be hospital food, but because Sharon credited the bag lunch Mark had made for Paul for her willingness to trust a too-handsome, too-well-groomed, too-mannish man—not to mention the suit and tie—on the day Paul had first wandered into Harbor Hospice.

"Some radish sprouts," Mark added.

"What's the goo?"

"Applesauce with a minced-up scallion."

Sharon pressed her sandwich back together. "I would happily divorce John and marry this sandwich. And we have to eat fast because he's coming by to take me to the airport soon."

It was news to Mark that Sharon was taking a two-week break from her gig in the ICU to work at the refugee camp in Lesbos, but it was not surprising. This was surely Paul's idea of a recruiting trip, and it really was Sharon's idea of a vacation.

Sharon said, "I should've thought to ask if you wanted me to bring something from you in case I see Paul."

This made Mark think he should've wanted to send something to Paul. A club chair? His car? Instead of mentioning these or any of the other items on the inane, panicky list of possibilities he came up with, he said, "Then I'd have to believe he wasn't here."

Sharon nodded.

Mark was going to add something about spring break overlooking the Piazza Navona, but that possibility seemed more remote than Paul's little trawler bobbing around in the middle of the Aegean Sea.

5.

It was snowing lightly when Mark left for Amherst on Saturday morning, and about fifteen minutes later, he was driving through a blizzard on the turnpike. The materteral navigation system in Paul's little black Audi was alerting Mark to hazardous road conditions ahead, and then his phone buzzed, first with a call he didn't catch, and then three texts. He couldn't pull over, as the snow was banked up in the emergency lane, and he knew the piles would only get deeper if he kept going west toward his childhood home in the Berkshires, a past he had relegated to the deep permafrost of his imagination after the controversy that erupted during his tenure at McClintock College, which briefly brought his long-dead father back into Mark's life.

His phone buzzed a few more times, so he took the next exit, and pulled into a gas station parking lot. The weather predictions for Western Massachusetts were dire—more than a foot of snow was on the way, along with winds exceeding sixty miles per hour. Mark's horizon was considerably brighter. The first of several texts he'd received announced the cancellation of the NEPCAJE meeting at Amherst. And though there was another storm brewing among participants attempting to settle on a plausible makeup date, after a couple of quick exchanges with the dean, Mark was allowed to opt out of that meeting by agreeing to deliver his literature review to the committee two weeks from today. He knew he ought to take advantage of his early dismissal and get right to work on his assignment, but instead he headed to Ipswich to check on the fate of the Saab.

Two hours later, Ozzie handed him his car keys. "It was nothing—a new ignition cylinder is all." Ozzie was keeping an eye on a young guy spreading snowmelt under the seven cars jammed into the service station's four parking spots.

"So it's fine," Mark said.

"You've got about three months left on those struts," Ozzie said. "And I sealed up the moon roof with caulk to stop that leak once and for all."

The leak was news to Mark—well, since the last repair. "So—don't open it for a while?"

"I disabled the switch," Ozzie said.

"But everything else?"

Ozzie didn't respond.

Mark said, "I mean, like the brakes."

"What about them?"

"I'm just asking," Mark said.

"If you have trouble stopping, let me know. Is that Paul's car you've got?" He turned and yelled, "Hey, Bobby, wanna take the Saab for a spin?" He turned to Mark. "Can you drop him back here?"

Mark said, "Of course."

Ozzie tossed the Saab keys to Bobby, who went to adjust the driver's seat. "Listen, I had him shovel you out," Ozzie said. "I'm trying to throw some work his way. I'd like him to learn he doesn't have to end up like his old man. Anyway, it's a pain in the ass to maneuver my plow in your drive-way. Same deal as always, I'll bill you. Kid can't hold on to a dollar, but he's a worker. He's my ex-wife's sister's stepkid."

Bobby followed Mark home, and then walked around to the passenger side of the Saab while Mark parked Paul's car. Unlike Ozzie, Bobby had shoveled off the front steps and porch, and a path to the oil pipe for the fur-nace on the other side of the house. When Mark complimented him on the work and handed him a tip, Bobby pulled his beanie down over his forehead and refused the cash.

"I'm not allowed to handle my own money right yet," he said.

A few minutes later, Mark asked if he'd grown up in Ipswich. He was thinking of the guy who had towed his Saab, wondering if a kid like Bobby would ever get the chance to see the possibility of being someone else, doing something he'd never imagined.

Bobby tugged his hat down a little further and mumbled that Ozzie was his uncle—sort of. Mark said Ozzie was sort of everybody's uncle, and Bobby closed his eyes, pressing himself against the door. His body finally relaxed when the garage was in sight, but he didn't jump out immediately as Mark stopped the car.

"I know it's really small and everything, Mr. Sternum," Bobby said, pulling off his hat, "but I like your house. Have a great day." He slammed the door and ran up to Ozzie in the office. Ozzie said something, and Bobby nodded, and then they gave each other a fist bump, a small but memorable graduation ceremony.

6.

Mark rarely heard from the Professor on weekends, but while he was sifting through the sections of the Sunday papers in Ipswich, before he'd had a chance to write his One Percent email to Paul, he found himself regaling the Professor with the futility of the drive to Amherst and complaining about the literature review he still hadn't even started to write. Mark also recounted his time watching that doctor in the ICU, who seemed to get by regurgitating the nurses' reviews of the patients, and though there was nothing extraordinary or even especially interesting about this from the Professor's perspective, Mark realized that he envied and maybe even admired the efficient way that doctor plagiarized authority while leaving the burden of accuracy—and liability—on the shoulders of the nurses who were charged with reading and interpreting the patients' symptoms. And though all of this was met with profound radio silence, so that Mark was basically talking to himself, he didn't relent until he had opened his laptop and found the file with the list of NEPCAJE books, hoping he could persuade the Professor to look it over and offer some perspective and advice about how Mark might make quick work of the task—if only, Mark added, so he could afford to devote as much time to those op-eds the Professor was writing as they surely deserved.

7.

After circling his desk for several hours on Sunday, occasionally sitting down to reread the list of book titles he was responsible for, Mark Googled his way into a wormhole of higher-education hysteria, where he remained until midnight, zigzagging around reviews and rebuttals and heated letters to editors that were as contradictory and contrary as the NEPCAJE books themselves. He still hadn't written a word when the last of the students' twelve Technical Exercises popped into his mailbox, so he bundled them up, printed copies for himself, and set aside a packet for the Professor. He didn't go to bed, and by six thirty on Monday morning, when it was obvious that sleep was not on the menu, he wandered down to Paul's office and rode the stationary bike for half an hour, not for the exercise but to spare himself the bother of inventing a better metaphor for his existence.

Mark experienced no adverse effects from the lack of sleep, though it occasioned some inconvenience for others. He was late getting to campus, and halfway to Hum Hall he had to go back to his car for his bag, which he later learned had left Anton, Isaac, and Jane marooned outside his office until a departmental secretary wandered by and told them Mark was attending the Curriculum Committee meeting, which by two fifteen was true because Althea Morgan had spotted him strolling past the windows of the first-floor conference room and collared him as he headed toward the stairs.

"The meeting started almost an hour ago, and I've been doing everything but card tricks to keep everyone in place so we can vote. We need a quorum. And you owe me this one, Mark."

Mark was trying to recall what question was on the ballot, but Althea seemed to think he was checking her math to measure his debt.

Taking hold of his sleeve, she said, "Remind me—how many classes are you teaching this semester?"

Althea had a damnably good memory and a thick file on everyone in the department to back her up when necessary. She had reluctantly agreed to be chair when she was first asked to take the five-year appointment. That was ten years ago. As no one else on the English faculty was willing to spend five days a week on campus dealing with the likes of the English faculty, she had effectively turned the department into Cuba—a haven for aging, would-be radicals whose loyalty could be bought on the cheap, a dreamy island effectively cut off from the rest of the world with a rapidly shrinking population and, when Mark cast his affirmative vote, the only undergraduate English major in the country that still required students to take two semesters of Shakespeare and two semesters of pre-Elizabethan literature.

The classroom was full and silent when Mark arrived a minute before three. All twelve heads were bowed over phones. Mark pulled out the packets of new stories so he wouldn't forget to hand them around.

Leo looked up and said, "You heard? There's been another attack in Paris."

Mark nodded, though he had not heard the news.

Someone said, "The guy is still on the loose."

Mark said, "So be careful out there. And be grateful we are here. Any questions about what was said in the short workshops about your hit-and-run stories?"

The phones disappeared, the packets appeared. And then nothing.

Mark let a few minutes pass. "Let's go through them in reverse order for a change."

Neither Willa nor Virginia had any questions.

Rashid said, "I had a lot of questions during my workshop, but now they just seem like—well not questions anymore, just issues I have to work out. The comments were really helpful."

Penelope passed, too.

It was Max's turn. "I hate to say it, but point proved."

Mark smiled.

Anton said, "What's the point?"

Max said, "All we wanted to do the first time we had to suffer silently during workshops was answer back to every comment, try to get somebody to tell you what you ought to do to make something work better, or just to get a better reaction. Now, when he takes off our gags, nobody has anything to say."

Anton looked up at Mark. "Was that your point?"

Mark said, "You aren't confused about anything you heard about your story, Anton?"

"I'm confused about how to fix it, but that's my problem."

"Bingo!" Max turned to Leo. "I dare you to come up with something about your story."

Leo turned to Julio. "I double-dare you."

Julio slapped his hands against the chest of his puffy parka. "I have two questions. Are we supposed to put our names on our annotated drafts of everybody else's stories?"

Mark said, "Yes."

Julio said, "Did everybody hear that?"

He got a few grudging nods in response.

Willa said, "And? Your second question?"

Julio said, "That was two."

Jane and Isaac passed.

Dorothy said, "Could we maybe admit defeat and talk about ideas for revising? I mean, I rewrote the monosyllable story—"

"Already?" This was Charles. "We can do that?"

"They're your stories," Mark said.

"Anyway," Dorothy said, "when Mark read it, he agreed—I think you did—that it was better."

"Much," Mark said. "The literal text felt more authoritative, more confident."

"But then you had four entirely new questions that didn't come up in my first draft, either in the typed comments or in workshop," Dorothy said.

"It's a new story to me every time," Mark said.

"Okay," Dorothy said, "so, how will I know when it is done?"

All heads turned to Mark.

"When the portfolio is due," Max said.

Mark didn't say anything.

Willa said, "Maybe you're never really done with a story."

Leo said, "I agree. You just stop at some point, and it's like, that's the painting because that's when you put down the brush."

"Or maybe when—" Rashid smiled.

Mark said, "When?"

"This doesn't really answer Dorothy's question, but I like what we talked about last time, how every story is a transaction. When I was writing the yard sale story—is it okay to talk about the new stories?"

"Please talk about something new," Max said.

"I spent hours thinking about currencies—you know, not just the money changing hands, but what else had to be, or could be exchanged."

Virginia said, "The emotional currencies."

"And the price of things," Penelope added. "I mean, the different value the buyer and the seller might put on an item."

"So you're saying if the transaction is complete, the story is complete?" Dorothy didn't sound convinced.

The discussion went on for almost an hour, until the Professor slipped in, and Dorothy said, "Well, thanks, everyone. I'm more confused than ever." She fixed her gaze on the fading afternoon beyond the unoccupied windowsills. "And before you say so, I know that makes you happy."

The Professor didn't say a word. He picked up a thick stack of paper and called out each of the twelve names, waiting each time for someone to look up or raise a hand, and then he slid another packet of three or four stapled pages down the table. "Read."

Mark looked at the one packet left in front of him.

ESSENTIAL TEXT

This is a pared-down version of the text of your original story. My intention was not to revise your story but to give you an editorial response based strictly on your prose choices—that is, based on what is here, rather than what is not here.

I am not proposing this as an alternative or as a more authoritative version of your text. I am hoping to open up your sense of the opportunities for revising your original draft.

My aim as I read and reread your yard sale story was to pare away words, phrases, or sentences that were not essential to my understanding of the literal text (the characters and action) and material that did not serve my understanding of your suggestive text. (You might well discover that there is more editing to do.) My hope is that this pared-down text will help you identify choices that are not working as you intended, as well as opportunities for heightening the effect of your most suggestive choices.

In a few instances, I moved phrases or sentences, rearranged the sequence, or transposed conversations. If I added a word or phrase, or altered a form of your chosen word, I put the new text in brackets. A quick glance at the few brackets will let you see how few words I altered or added.

What is here is your voice, and your choices: your essential text.

I don't expect you to adopt this version of your story when you revise. I simply wanted you to see which elements of your literal and suggestive texts were essential to my understanding of your intent. You might well want to eliminate additional text, you might want to restore some material I undervalued, and you will certainly want to invent some new action and dialogue to deepen and complicate the central character and to more potently and poignantly deliver the suggestive truth of the transaction for both your characters and your reader.

The next page is simply your essential text, and on the following pages you can see exactly what was edited away from your original. My hope is that you will see that the most reliable way to revise—I mean, the one thing you can do when you are confused about readers' responses and not yet confident about your own sense of the story—is to cut, cut, cut. I suggest you choose an arbitrary percentage and eliminate words and phrases until you reach that percentage. Then, read what remains—your essential text.

In all of these drafts, I aimed to cut at least 40 percent.

* * *

(Mark Sternum / 498 words originally; 245 essential words)

The Professor had tomato plants on the passenger seat, [but] one table [at] the yard [sale] was piled high with books. As he pulled over, two young guys loaded a mountain bike missing its front wheel into a black Cadillac.

The books were of no interest—college texts, an encyclopedia of music—nor were the harmonica, keyboard, or the banjo in a black case lined with satin.

Two stout women wrestl[ed] with a tent, glancing at the bearish man inside the garage.

A blonde yelled, "Richard!" [from] a picnic table, her hand on a cash box.

Richard stepped into the light. He was wearing an Oberlin sweatshirt, holding a bent bicycle wheel.

As she approached, the blonde—Richard's wife?—grabbed the bent wheel. "Let it go."

Richard sidled up to the Professor. "Buy the harmonica." His breath smelled boozy.

The Professor said, "I don't play."

Richard slid two twenties under the harmonica and whispered, "Follow me."

Richard's wife said the [women] could have [the tent] for forty.

One of the[m] found a sleeping bag inside the tent. "It's warm," she said. "Creepy."

The Professor followed Richard to the picnic table, handed him the cash and the harmonica. "I don't want this."

Richard pressed the harmonica to his lips, and then pocketed it. He yelled, "Sold!" and waved the twenties for his wife to see. His eyes were teary. "So awfully quiet around here."

The Professor headed for his car, hoping his young seedlings weren't dead.

* * *

The Professor ~~typically slowed as he drove past yard sales only to marvel at the junk people considered valuable. But it was June, sunny at last, and instead of inchoate student stories on the passenger seat, he~~ had a flat of tomato plants on the passenger seat, [but]. ~~Plus,~~ one table [at]~~in~~ the yard [sale] was piled high with books. As he pulled over, two young guys loaded a mountain bike missing its front wheel into a~~n old~~ black Cadillac ~~that looked like a hearse.~~

The books were ~~handsome, hardbound, and~~ of no interest—college text~~books~~, an encyclopedia of ~~American~~ music~~--~~, ~~biographies of Papa This, Joe That, and other apparently admirable and dead bluegrass pioneers. There was also a~~ nor were the silver harmonica~~,~~ ~~someone thought was worth $40, an electronic~~ keyboard, ~~and a~~ or the banjo in a black case lined with ~~red~~ satin.

~~More interesting were t~~Two stout women ~~— lesbians?~~ —wrestl~~ing~~ed with a~~n old Boy Scout~~ tent, ~~both~~ glancing ~~beseechingly~~ at the ~~big,~~ bearish man ~~on a lawn chair~~ inside the garage.

~~From across the patchy brown lawn, a~~A blonde yelled, "Richard!" [from]~~She was at~~ a picnic table, her hand on a cash box. ~~She headed toward the garage.~~

Richard stepped ~~out~~ into the light ~~and winced~~. He was wearing a[n] ~~too-small~~ Oberlin sweatshirt, holding a bent bicycle wheel.

As she approached, the blonde—Richard's wife~~?, surely~~—said, "That bike is finally gone," ~~and~~ grabbed the bent wheel. "~~You have to l~~Let it go." ~~As she passed the Professor on her way to the tent, she said, "How about fifteen for the encyclopedia?"~~

Richard sidled up to the Professor~~. and whispered, "Do me a favor?" His breath smelled boozy.~~ "Buy the harmonica."

The Professor said, "I don't play."

~~The two guys who'd bought the bike were back, pounding on the unplugged keyboard, as if by sheer force they could bring it back to life.~~

Richard slid two twenties under the harmonica and whispered, "Follow me." ~~As he walked toward the picnic table, he paused and lowered the lid on the banjo.~~

~~By then, the tent was open.~~ Richard's wife said ~~it was priced at fifty, but~~ the ~~lesbians~~ [women] could have ~~it~~[the tent] for forty.

One of the[m] ~~lesbians~~ found a sleeping bag inside the tent. "It's warm," she said. "~~Sort of c~~Creepy."

~~Richard's wife said, "Twenty five?" She sounded desperate or irate when she said, "It's all going for a music scholarship."~~

———— ~~The lesbians hightailed it to their car.~~

———— ~~The young guys seemed to be eyeing the two twenties, so the~~ The Professor followed Richard to the picnic table, handed him the cash and the harmonica. "I don't want this."

Richard ~~closed his eyes,~~ pressed the harmonica to his lips ~~for few seconds~~, and then pocketed it. He yelled, "Sold!" and waved the twenties for his wife to see. His eyes were teary. "So awfully quiet around here."

The Professor ~~decided Richard was drunk. To mollify him, and to amuse himself, he said, "You drive a hard bargain," and~~ headed for his car, hoping his young seedlings weren't dead.

(Mark Sternum: 498 words originally; 245 essential words)

When Mark looked up, all twelve windowsills were occupied. Sighs and hums occasionally rippled through the silence, and soon gave way to *so much better, can't even tell where he cut until I look at the other pages, 60 percent shorter but at least now it has an ending, I didn't know you could start with the guy already looking at stuff in the yard, so much better it's almost like somebody else wrote it.*

"Are we going to bother to have workshops on Wednesday?" This was Dorothy.

Leo said, "Good question. Why listen to people talk about all the stuff I shouldn't have bothered to write in the first place?"

The Professor said, "Everyone will read the first drafts. Only the writer will have read the essential-text version I prepared—which is not my idea of the authoritative text but my sense of what works best, what matters most in your original. Other readers, I trust, will confirm or contradict or otherwise complicate my reading. So, please take a packet of all twelve stories on your way out."

Mark said, "Jane? Maybe Anton? And—someone else was hoping to see me in office hours."

"I was." Isaac was still flipping back and forth from his original to his essential text. "But this sort of answers my question about how to start revising."

"I'll be in my office on Wednesday."

Jane and Anton nodded.

Max said, "I always end up leaving this class feeling insulted and grateful. Is that Stockholm syndrome?"

"The death toll in Paris is up to nineteen," Dorothy said.

Rashid waved. "If I came by Wednesday on the later side—two o'clock, or so—would that be okay?"

"I'd be sorry if you didn't," Mark said. "Knock to let me know you've arrived."

The Professor said, "Enough. Take a packet and go away."

As the classroom emptied out, Mark flipped back through the briefer and admittedly more promising draft of his yard sale story the Professor had prepared. He didn't countenance every edit—he missed the identifiable lesbians and thought their discovery of the sleeping bag was more potent when a reader had a fix on their identities. But the essential text made it clear that the central characters needed more clearly inscribed arcs than he'd provided in his draft, and it was inarguably true that he could now choose 250 new words to etch those into the story. What surprised Mark more, more even than the Professor's advance delivery of the annotated drafts of all thirteen stories this week, was the second, thicker packet beneath his essential-text packet.

Mark read the cover page a couple of times. He had to admit it was clever.

You are the attending physician. The NEPCAJE books are the patients. The many nurses have done the hard work of carefully reading, considering, and reviewing each patient's presenting problems and progress.

Save your precious time for what really matters.

What followed were twenty-five pages of a perfectly noncontroversial literature review. Mark was impressed. The Professor had simply copied the titles on the NEPCAJE reading list, opened up a page of space beneath each one and, with the addition of a few introductory sentences and connecting clauses, inserted reviews from professional journals, major newspapers, and even a few incomprehensible foreign-language publications, which aptly and authoritatively and irreproachably summed up the central argument made by each author and the counterarguments that had bubbled up in the wake of its publication.

Attached to the NEPCAJE literature review were four additional pages, a windy and rather pompous first draft of an op-ed that the Professor was hoping to send to the *New York Times* by the beginning of next week, as well as a parenthetical threat about imminent delivery of the first sixty-five pages of a novel that was well underway.

FOUR

1.

Jane, Anton, and Virginia were seated on the floor outside his office when Mark arrived a few minutes before one o'clock on Wednesday. Max was a few office doors down from them, perched like a bird on an upturned recycling bin, hugging his legs, chin resting on his knees, eyes closed, ears plugged into something, his blond plumage gathered on top of his head with a rubber band and splayed out like a little cockscomb.

Two doors opened across the hall. Alan Truemay, whose Chaucer seminar started halfway across campus just about now, backed out of his office, surveyed the hallway, and clucked his disapproval at the students camping out in his backyard. He was built like a broomstick, and he had long cultivated an image in the department as a misanthrope, which was his attempt to take credit for being disliked. He kept one hand on the wall as he inched down the hall and said something to his shoes about building codes and fire laws, as if students were a safety hazard.

No one emerged from the other open door. Rita Jebdi also had a one o'clock class, but Mark knew from former students that her Romantic Poets course was widely known as The Late Romantics.

Anton said, "Jane's first."

"Oh, I don't mind waiting," Jane said, but she slapped down the cover of some tome—one of the Russians, Mark guessed—brushed back her red hood, and stood up quickly, pulling a piece of paper from her satchel as she sped past the others. "Maybe we should start with this." She handed Mark a revision of her yard sale story. She sat down.

Mark read the first few lines.

"And if it's okay with you, I'd also like to discuss my idea—not my idea, because I know you don't approve of us having ideas, but my strategy? Maybe I mean my approach? I'd like to get your permission before I waste too much time."

Mark looked up. "Permission for what?"

"Oh, keep reading for now, and then we'll talk."

Mark said, "Any other instructions?"

"No, no, not unless you would like me to explain why I shifted the yard sale to Buck's County. I have been there. More than once. It's a famous part of Pennsylvania."

Mark said, "Anything else?"

"You did make a big deal about specific place names in class."

Either she was tone-deaf or obnoxious. It was often hard to tell with students. Mark said, "You sound aggrieved."

"I do?" Her freckles disappeared beneath a flashflood of a blush. She was either ashamed about her performance so far or embarrassed that she didn't know the definition of *aggrieved*. Another tricky distinction.

"Are you nervous, Jane?"

"So." She shrank a few inches and shook her head. "My stories seem so stupid compared to everything else in the class. I'm getting a lot of criticism in workshops. I mean, I know I missed a few things we already went over in class, like place names. But why does that make me seem greedy? Is that what you just called me?"

"No." Mark turned away and put her revision on his desk, waiting until he was sure his smile had faded. He spelled *aggrieved* for her, and as she took notes, he explained that she'd sounded annoyed, as if she felt his urging her to be specific in her fiction was unfair.

"I've never even heard that word before." Again, she sounded aggrieved. She studied the notes she'd taken. "Are you sure that's how it's spelled?"

So, maybe she was tone-deaf and obnoxious. "Pretty sure," Mark said. He had intended to reassure her about the quality of her short stories, but now he was leaning toward a lecture on her attitude. Instead, he grabbed her revision. "I want to read this aloud to you." It was tempting to provide etiquette lectures, psychological counseling, and even romantic advice during office hours, as it was tempting to devote class time to propagandizing for any number of political, cultural, and social causes—and not only because it required no preparation, no genuine engagement, no effort at all. After a few minutes in an office or a few hours in a classroom, it was easier to pretend you knew a young woman well enough to diagnose her attitude and correct her behavior than it was to accept that what was actually between you, all you really shared, was a story you had requested and she had delivered. Mark said, "I'll stop and make a few notes for you to think about later, and you should also take notes on anything that doesn't seem to work as you intended."

He started in immediately, and so did Jane, who proved to be the much harsher critic.

Her diagnosis: nothing happens during the first half of the story, and the second half is so rushed it's impossible to follow.

Mark's diagnosis: Maybe a bit too much of the *hello*, and *my name is*, and *oh, hello, there, my name is*, and *how are you*, and other procedural dialogue that readers didn't need. And there were also at least three wordy exchanges about *how much is that* followed by *that costs this much in dollars* followed by *will you accept this much in dollars for that,* all of which could be better accomplished with a few price tags and a simply stated counteroffer, like *Thirty?* "By my quick count," Mark added, "you could cut about fifty words that way."

"Oh, easily," Jane said, a little smugly.

Mark said, "Now, you've got three minutes to ask your other question."

"It's about using one of the Technical Exercises—expanding it into my first full-length story." Jane had pulled out a folder and rearranged its contents as she spoke. "I mean, is that going to be original enough for you?"

Mark said, "Is it original enough for you?"

"I guess that depends," she said.

"I agree," Mark said.

That seemed to satisfy her. She stuck her folder into her satchel and stood up. "Who should I tell to come in next?"

Mark said, "Let them figure that out," and ushered Jane into the hall as Virginia walked in.

"I won't take up too much time, I promise." To prove her point, she dropped her suede pouch onto the seat of the alumni chair and dug out two pieces of paper. "I revised two of my stories. I hope they're better. I think they are. I kind of lose track of my original train of thought, what I thought I was writing about, I mean, because sometimes I'm so interested in some particular thing we talked about in class, like suggestive language, or even those—contractions?"

Mark sat down at his desk. "Conjunctions."

"Why would I call them contractions?" With her braids and headband, she looked like the poster girl for a Happening, circa 1969.

Mark said, "Did you want to give those revisions to me?"

She did, but she was hoping Mark would read them later—"any time you feel like it, and if not, that's fine, too"—so she could come back next Wednesday to go over them before class. As she handed over her revised stories, she said, "Do you grade us on effort?"

Mark thought, As opposed to? But he didn't say so, not least of all because the Professor considered effort irrelevant and accused Mark of behaving like Santa Claus at the end of every semester. Fortunately, Mark didn't have to say anything.

Virginia was also wondering—this required another dive into her suede bag, though she came up empty-handed—if Mark would read an application essay she was writing for a dance fellowship, which she promised to find and email to him before their meeting, or else she was going to end up in the MFA program at the University of Maryland.

Mark said, "Is that not a good thing?"

"It's good because it's pretty near Annapolis, where my girlfriend is."

Mark said, "At the Naval Academy?"

Virginia nodded.

Mark said, "Wow."

Virginia said, "Right?" She dove in to her bag one more time. No luck. Her girlfriend had another year at Annapolis, and the MFA program was three years long, and who knew where the girlfriend would be while she worked off the five additional years she owed the navy? "And that's only if you don't suspect she is secretly hoping to stick it out for twenty years or more," which Virginia clearly did, though if someone offered her the chance to be in a dance company for twenty years, she'd probably take it, so fair was fair. And could they also maybe talk about how she was doing grade-wise next week?

Anton was next, and he was all business, having discovered a raft of new conjunctions for his monosyllabic story, some of which were conjunctions. He was surprised to learn that *then* was not a conjunction but an adverb, and he was aggrieved when Mark told him that *next* could be an adjective, adverb, a noun, or a preposition, but not a conjunction.

"Basically, everything but the one thing I want it to be?"

Mark said, "Just about."

Anton said, "I started writing a story about a person." He let it go at that for a long while. He wasn't dragging around the car coat today, but he did have a new sweater—a black wool turtleneck, which looked warm, but made him look jaundiced and deathly thin.

Mark said, "I like stories about people."

"He's sick," Anton said. He leaned down and rolled up the cuffs of his jeans, exposing the flannel lining. To reassure Mark? To provoke a sartorial comment?

"People do get sick," Mark said. "Who's telling the story?"

"What do you mean?"

"Is it first-person? Or is there a narrator?"

Anton had to think about that. "You know, you're right. I should have made a better choice about that. Right now, the guy is telling the story. But what about having a narrator who's omniscient, you mean?"

"Depends on what you want us to know, what you want us to discover as we read. By way of—"

"I know, I know, by way of example, not as a suggestion. I must've read that in your typed-out comments on my stories ten times by now." Anton turned over the annotated draft of his revision, and pointed a pen at the blank page. "So, what's your example?"

"By way of example, and not as a suggestion for you to adopt," Mark said, "the narrator might be another character in the story, someone who doesn't know everything, someone who might not know or understand anything about the person who is ill."

Anton said, "So it could be first-person, but that other person would be the storyteller?"

"Right. Or you might want to use third person-limited."

"Of course! Like that yard sale story. We're limited to the buyer—in my story, the guy who is not sick—but we're actually more interested in the guy who is sick."

"Or neither. Maybe what occasions the intersection of their lives is the real story. Maybe the illness is not the heart of the story."

"What's the transaction? What's the currency?" Anton was writing furiously.

Mark said, "Are you sure the other guy is not sick?"

Anton giggled. "I didn't actually know there was another guy till I sat down. Would it be okay if I left now and just went to work on this before class?"

Mark said, "Goodbye."

Anton said, "Goodbye."

Before Mark sat down, Rashid knocked on his open door. She was wearing an ivy-vined off-white headscarf and something belted at the waist that looked like silk pajamas.

"Come in."

Rashid backed up a few steps into the hall. "Wouldn't you like a few minutes to yourself?"

"I spend way too much time with myself," Mark said. "Take a seat."

Rashid sat at attention in the alumni chair. Good manners, or just good posture?

"Thank you for seeing me, Mark."

Mark said, "I really prefer to have visitors during office hours." It was not impossible to imagine that Rashid had been a young man—Persian, Mark guessed—and was now transitioning toward her true self as a young Muslim woman. Or perhaps the headscarves were just part of a strategy to deflect curiosity from gender to religion or ethnicity. Or maybe she was a young Iranian Muslim woman. Or a young American woman with an olive complexion and a soft spot for silk? All suggestive, nothing definitive.

Rashid said she was struggling with her revisions, and she had decided not to bring any of them with her today. She looked even more beset when Mark reminded her that she didn't have to revise all three of the Technical Exercises, that is was up to her whether she chose to revise one, two, or all three to include in her final portfolio.

"One way or another, we're always forced to choose for this class," Rashid said. "It's not at all what I expected when I signed up for creative writing."

Mark said, "Is it frustrating?"

"Very," Rashid said, and smiled for the first time. "I'm sure that makes you happy."

Mark said, "Does it make you happy?"

"Not really," Rashid said. "But I get the sense you're not trying to make us happy—like with your notes on our stories. I mean I am very happy they're typed—so grateful to get something from a professor that I can actually read for a change. But they are so detailed, and they make me so aware of what my story isn't, the opportunities I didn't even notice. And then it's all back on me. I mean, I hope you know I love our class, except when I realize I have to start a new story or try to revise one of the old ones. And then it's choose, choose, choose all over again. It's like trying to decide what to cook for dinner while you're standing in the middle of Whole Foods."

Of course, that was exactly what people who weren't served their meals in cafeterias and restaurants did before they cooked dinner. Instead of pursuing the home economics lesson, though, Mark said, "Thus, the utility of limits. I mean, if you have only $20, and you can only shop from three aisles in Whole Foods, and you have to feed twelve people—well, suddenly, the choices are not so many, and the meal has already begun to take shape. You won't be springing for lobster, for starters."

"It's hard to do that—not only to impose limits, but to love them, like you want us to."

"It's hard to remember that one story is not every story, that every meal is just one of many meals you will prepare. And the more carefully you choose and arrange the specific ingredients for the one meal, the more memorable it will be."

"You would get along with my grandmother," Rashid said. "She says bad cooks like to use every spice in Bombay. Could I show you something I've been working on?"

So, maybe she was Hindu? "Please," Mark said.

Rashid handed him two typed pages. "I've been thinking about currencies and transactions a lot. I hope it's okay, but I've used your scenario as the basis—the history, really—for what's there."

"I think all stories are retold stories," Mark said. "Do you have a sense of how long your story ought to be when it's done?"

"I've set a limit of two thousand words," Rashid said. "I think you have almost five hundred words there. It's in third-person omniscient—I hope. Past tense. It takes place in Dallas, but I haven't figured out yet how to get that into the opening lines without it sounding like an announcement."

It was a superb start, and though it was really unclear how she was going to bring it to completion in fewer than five thousand words, the prose was almost flawless. What Mark understood so far was that the central character was a married woman—Chandi—whose child had fallen to his death during an elementary school field trip. In the immediate aftermath, Chandi had been unnerved and appalled by the words and behavior of the mothers of her child's classmates when they came by to offer consolation in the form of coffee cakes and casseroles. These mothers and their baked goods had appeared in Rashid's Technical Exercise about the yard sale. But in this expanded version of the story, Chandi had purchased a large freezer chest to preserve all of that food, which she was preparing to dole out to those same mothers when the ideal—preferably awful—occasions arose.

"It's sublime," Mark said, "and hauntingly sad. That freezer she keeps opening and closing—it's as if she'd got her kid's body in a private morgue in her basement."

Rashid looked delighted. "I don't know yet if her husband even knows it's there. And Chandi might—"

"I don't want to hear it," Mark said. "I want to read it."

Rashid nodded and stood. "We're only allowed to bring in the first five hundred words for next week?"

Mark said, "The goal is to keep it short for those initial workshops so we can give everyone a sense of what we see in their opening sequences—what's at stake, where we sense each story is going, and what opportunities we're hoping will be explored." As she opened the door to leave, Mark said, "If you named the elementary school—Dallas Central, for example—wouldn't that be a simple way to get readers located geographically? And it's organic, as the school figures in the text already."

Rashid leaned into the threshold, and then turned back to Mark. "Whole Foods, organic aisle," she said, and then she disappeared.

Mark leaned back in his chair. All this, all this, and still half an hour till class time.

The students didn't yet know what was happening, but several of them had sensed it, the turning of the great tide, the receding of their expectations for the semester, the ebbing of the familiar. Some of them had already begun to venture offshore, diving and bobbing in the deep, cold, roiling waters, stirring up something new, something fresh, something original that they were eager to bring ashore. There were still a few feet of beach to be uncovered as the semester ebbed toward its midpoint, and a couple of the students were still splashing in the warm, shallow tidal pools of the familiar that would be the last to drain away. But even they would eventually surrender to the incoming tide, or they'd be knocked over by a big, fresh wave and get dragged into the depths along with everyone else. It was not always gratifying, and it was rarely accomplished without some trauma or tantrums, but it was inevitable. All that varied year to year was the tidal range, the distance between what had to be drained away, let go, and the quantity and force of what rolled in. And it was inevitable that soon Mark would not be leading them but standing back, receiving what they discovered on each foray into the open ocean, retreating farther and farther with each new advancing rush, ceding more and more territory, sometimes running to a height of land just to keep from being swamped until he was so far away that the offshore swimmers lost sight of him entirely.

Mark might have imagined his way right through class, if not the rest of the semester, but someone was singing, someone who could really sing.

2.

As Mark walked out into the hallway, so did two other people he didn't recognize. Adjuncts? Max was still perched on the recycling bin, still plugged in to something—presumably, some musical accompaniment. His head flitted back and forth a few times, and then he pulled out his plugs and waved both hands apologetically at the two scowling adjuncts, who retreated to their subleased offices and slammed the doors.

Mark said, "Have you been waiting all this time to see me?"

Max didn't move. "Yes and no."

"Was that really you singing?"

Max said, "It was Top."

Mark didn't say anything.

Max said, "Baritone in *The Tender Land*."

Mark said, "Copland?"

Max smiled. "Aaron Copland. I can come back some other day."

Mark said, "I'm good now. Or you could just come in and sing for a while."

Max stood up, took a big breath, and in a deep, booming baritone that made his little cockscomb flutter, he sang, "If it's stories you want, I know a few myself," and then tipped the recycling bin right-side up and followed Mark into his office.

Max got himself seated in the Lotus Position in the alumni chair. He looked about ten years old.

Mark said, "You have an astonishing voice, Max. Was that line you sang about stories Top?"

Max nodded. "Might be my favorite role—well, not including Figaro." He let out a long, slow breath, and flexed his spine. "And I just now heard I didn't get the part. The Music Department is doing a big production with the Conservatory in Boston. Even the guy who got the part knows he can't really do it, but that's show biz—one of those clichés you love so much."

"Still, a disappointment," Mark said.

"Or just sour grapes," Max said, briefly delighted to have come up with another cliché. And then his demeanor darkened. "Really, the guy who got it is a tenor. His pitch drops right out on half of Top's best stuff. But he's six-something, and I'm five two with two pairs of socks on, and please don't tell me I can become a voice teacher or the choral director at a summer camp or try out for community-theater musicals or give piano lessons in my spare time."

Mark said, "Agreed." Max was handsome, sophisticated, quick-witted, gifted with a beautiful voice, and smaller than most men. It was no use pretending it wasn't true or that it was a riddle Mark or anyone else could solve for him. "Did you want to talk to me about something else?"

"Well, I just now started my first story." Max strummed his cockscomb. "It's autobiographical. It's called, 'The Little Engine That Couldn't.'" He lifted his gaze and stared out the window.

Mark said, "I'd rather read a story about the other guy, the tenor who got the part." He waited until Max looked his way. "'The Big Engine That Shouldn't.'"

Max nodded and nodded, and finally grinned. He was giggling when he said, "'Can You Top This?'" He reached into his shirt pocket and pulled out a folded-up page. "So, I've been revising the second Technical Exercise for a while now, the hit-and-run and the 125-word sentence?"

His was memorable. "With the two brothers in the car?"

"And the terrible stuff in the bar in Part II, with them feeling sorry for themselves, which is all gone now."

"Good thinking," Mark said. "Am I allowed to read it?"

Max handed over the page. "Can I ask you a personal question first?"

"You can ask," Mark said.

Max pulled the rubber band from his hair and brushed the whole mess back with both hands. "When you write, do you really think about limits and trying to love them?"

"I really do." It was true. "If I'm not assigned a word limit for a column or an essay, I invent one. When I'm, say, writing a novel, I set a word limit for each chapter so I have a clear sense of how much space and time there is for me to get done what needs to get done. Why, Max? Does it seem somehow false to you?"

"No. It did, at first. I thought it was a trick or—you know, just a puzzle for us to work on. But what you said about *art* being cognate with *artifice* and *artificial*, well, that's gone a long way with me. Because it's one thing to accept the limits that are imposed on you, or even the limits you invent yourself, but it really is something else again to love them."

It was not clear if he was talking about his story or his life, whether he was thinking about Technical Limits—word count, verb tense, point of view—or lived limits—his limited height, that tall tenor's limited baritone range.

"I'm going to read this aloud, and I'll pause to make a few notes as I do," Mark said.

"Could I borrow a pen and some paper, then? I must have left my folder somewhere." Max unknotted his legs, rested his feet on the front rung of the chair.

Mark handed him a pad and a pen, and midway through Part II of Max's story, he stopped. "Oh, Max, this is genuinely elegant. I just understood the syntax. After that long sentence in Part I, where we see the narrator—the older one—persuade his younger brother to drive away from the body in the road, and then see him come to understand what he has done in the silence as they drive home, he loses his nerve, and they don't speak of it for almost a week, right? That's why in Part II, he starts so tentatively with, *Oh. Don't go. Not yet, bro.* One, two, three words—and each sequential sentence in Part II is one word longer than the last." Mark read to the end of the story. In the final sentence, the older brother confidently and viciously parodies his younger brother's threat to go to the police. "That last sentence is what? Twelve or thirteen words long?"

Max said, "Fifteen. Part II is 120 words total, I think."

"That last sentence seems really long after those abbreviated first three or four sentences, so it echoes the long sentence in Part I—not only the tone but the distended syntax. The older brother has found his voice again."

Max said, "And his nerve."

"It's a real coup, Max."

"What about that rhyme?" Max pointed to something in his notes. "When you were reading aloud, that *Don't go. Not yet, bro.* sounded a little cheesy."

"I'm not a huge fan of that *bro*, but I do sort of like the rhyme, the way it alerted me to the staccato rhythm of the syntax. More importantly, you might consider giving the younger brother a more compelling physical presence in Part II so the narration doesn't register as a soliloquy. Even if the kid sneezed or tied his shoe, it would help establish him as real. And in Part I, you might want to rethink that long clause set off with dashes, which isn't working as you intended. You want a sense of the car crash intruding into that moment, I think, but the dash actually prepares readers."

Max flipped over the notebook page and wrote for a few silent minutes.

The office door swung open, and in walked Anton. He'd come by with a question, but on the way he'd found a folder in the hall, which Mark told him to hand to Max, who tore off his page of notes and reflexively handed Mark's notebook to Anton.

Mark said, "That's mine. What's your question?"

Max said, "It's almost three."

Anton said, "It's starting to snow again."

Mark stood up and said, "And the question is?"

Max said, "Why didn't we all go to college in Florida?"

Anton said, "I thought it was going on two o'clock."

Mark hustled the two of them out of his office and watched them amble down the hall, one too short, one too sick. He followed them to the classroom, where he would not heal them or even console them but only close the door, shut out the world in which they found themselves wanting, not to help them escape it but to give them a chance to understand all it meant to have limits, to need limits, to choose our limits, to be defined by those limits, and to learn to love them.

3.

The classroom was uncommonly quiet when Mark arrived, and except for a couple of nods and a smile from Penelope, Mark's unpacking didn't disrupt the stillness. He took off his watch. He had two minutes to spare. He sat down, which did draw a few expectant glances his way.

"Oh, hi." This was Dorothy. "I didn't hear you come in. I was just reading an email from my adviser telling me my thesis is due the week we come back from spring break."

"I got the same email," Rashid said. "Are you in Comp Lit?"

"Government," Dorothy said, and then turned to Mark. "And I have a Statistics midterm in about ten seconds."

"I thought that wasn't till March," Julio said, scrolling madly on his phone.

Someone said, "It is almost March."

"Everything is happening at once," Dorothy said.

Isaac said, "Tell me about it."

Jane said, "We're not allowed to tell anything in here unless we write it down."

Max said, "*Down* is superfluous in that sentence."

Charles said, "What is the date today?"

Mark said, "Right question. I want to start with some scheduling issues, including dates for the story workshops for the rest of the semester, and then I want to add to your woes by reminding you that the first five hundred words of your first original stories are due in class one week from today, and a week or so after that, each of you will have a completed draft of that first story for us to read." It was surprising, but saying so would make it so. He sent around a two-sided photocopy. "You're going to take this away, look at your schedules for the rest of the semester, choose a couple of plausible dates for your first story workshop, and then turn over the page and choose a couple of plausible dates for your second story workshop. Next week, we'll finalize dates for everyone. You get it—this is your chance to avoid having too much due on a single day."

Jane said, "What are those dates in parentheses supposed to mean?"

Penelope said, "That's when the drafts are due in class." She held up her photocopy and pointed to a line, which she read: "Thirteen copies are due at the class before the workshop."

Jane didn't look grateful for the clarification.

Mark said, "That's to give the rest of us plenty of time to read and think about the drafts before the workshops."

Julio said, "So we have to make our own copies from now on?"

"Unless that's a financial burden for anyone, who can simply be in touch with me," Mark said.

Anton said, "Are we having class on Monday?"

Leo said, "It's Presidents' Day."

Anton said, "Which presidents?"

Dorothy said, "Can we talk about something other than the future?"

Virginia said, "It says on the syllabus that our class meets Wednesday and Thursday next week."

"Not Monday?" Anton again.

Isaac had rediscovered his copy of the syllabus, and he held it up. "It says here that portfolios are due on the last day of the semester, but do we just drop them off or do we have to stay for a whole class on that day?"

The Professor had turned up, and Mark was embarrassed to imagine what the melee sounded like to him. "At four thirty today in this very classroom, I am holding a seminar for anyone and everyone who has any question whatsoever about any scheduling concern or any date between now and the end of time," Mark said. "Presently, what should we say about the yard sale stories?"

This was met with a host of squints, awkward smiles, and flipping pages. The windowsills were empty. The Professor's decision to give back the edited, essential texts before today's brief workshops simply because he'd gotten them done quickly had been a mistake. It made the students feel their responses were pointless. But the Professor was content, as usual, to let Mark repair the damage.

Mark could see that the margins of most pages in the packets around the table were crammed with notes and suggestions, so he let the silence go for almost four minutes, hoping someone would risk a comment, and then he decided to let it go for another sixty seconds.

"Okay, okay," Dorothy said. "But why do I always end up talking first?"

Max said, "You might think that's a rhetorical question, but there is an answer."

Dorothy said, "Anyway," very slowly. She flipped to a new page in her packet and deliberately pressed down the fold at the top corner with her fist. "I only found two stories that used suggestion really successfully—I mean, I understood a child had died, and the writer didn't give me any obvious hints."

Penelope said, "Well, Rashid's for sure is one."

"Those horrible women with the casseroles," Dorothy said. "What else is there to say?"

This got a lot of approving murmurs and nods.

"And though I hate to admit it," Dorothy said, "that tire swing that the wind keeps moving in Max's story—that's the most memorable image for me in all of the stories."

"It's like a ghost," Anton said.

"Haunting," the Professor said.

"At the risk of sounding like a toady," Max said, "I actually think Dorothy is the only one who made sense of the financial transaction. Rashid and

I both sort of blew it off. But when the seller takes the bills and just tosses them aside after all that haggling with the buyer, you really feel something hopeless, how empty that currency is for her."

Jane said, "But I don't think you'd know it was a kid who died in Dorothy's story."

Max said, "If she just made that bicycle a tricycle, I think you would."

"You're right," Dorothy said. "Why didn't I think of that?"

Mark looked quickly at Max to prevent another rhetorical response.

"I loved Willa's music box," Penelope said. "And hers was the only story with a child as the buyer, which was genuinely suggestive."

"But do you think the kid sounds too—something?" Willa asked.

"I think maybe her speech is too poignant occasionally," Mark said.

The Professor said, "Does she have to be so responsive to questions from the adults? One of the challenges of writing dialogue for children is avoiding sentimentality, and one of the most provocative characteristics of children is their propensity for not behaving predictably or even sensibly. I'm actually a fan of a lot of the choices Willa makes, but I think that kid can be more provocative for readers, so we are made more aware of how odd the seller is."

Mark said, "I think you intend for us to see that the seller is reserved and almost emotionally comatose. Is that right?"

"Exactly," Willa said. "I have to work on the little girl."

Jane said, "I didn't get that at all. To me, the seller just seemed calm and controlled."

"She's pale, and she keeps trying to ignore that little girl, though," Leo said, "like she can't tolerate seeing a child that isn't her own."

"I don't see that," Jane said.

Virginia thought Leo's was the most successful story. "You don't really know a child died, but the yard sale seems so real," she said.

"The sense of place is also lovely in Leo's," Mark said, "and those circling clouds that the seller worries might bring a hurricane or some other disaster—that's terrific work."

The Professor said, "I could do without that empty picture frame."

"Hint, hint," Leo said. "It's gone."

Julio said, "What about the sticker with the kid's name on—"

"Gone," Leo said.

Penelope thought Julio and Anton did the best job of making the buyer the central character. "Each of them has a genuine reason for being there—not just for shopping, but for shopping for something inexpensive."

Rashid agreed, and she wondered if Anton had considered giving his buyer a son instead of a nephew, to simplify the suggestive connection to the seller. And so it went for another half hour. Only the windowsills behind Jane and Charles remained unoccupied. Their stories had been largely ignored. Mark had scribbled down a couple of things to ask about each, but the Professor suddenly asked everyone to pass the annotated drafts back to the writers.

Penelope said, "Could we maybe spend just the last few minutes talking about our original stories? They are due at the next class meeting."

Anton said, "That's Wednesday, not Monday, right?"

The Professor said, "What is there to say? Don't start your story with an alarm clock waking the central character. If you think you have a tremendous, devilishly surprising twist ending—make that revelation the first sentence of your story."

As it became clear that he wasn't going to leave it at that, the students dutifully took notes as he rattled off an endless assortment of proscriptions—no stories set on Venus; no stories miraculously narrated by pets; beware the wizened elder and the crazy but prophetic homeless person on the subway; and did he already say no zombies?

Mark could tell that he was just getting warmed up. He saw that Charles was not taking notes, and Jane was taking offense at almost every newly banned story element. Isaac was also looking a little dazed. And though the Professor had decided at the end of last semester that they should not continue to offer students the option of writing a longer Technical Exercise in lieu of the first original story, Mark now regretted his capitulation. Even if they chose not to write it, the elaborate scenario for that optional Technical Exercise gave students a practical way to understand the advice about starting a story in medias res and developing a suggestive subplot. But there was too little time today to rectify that error.

The Professor paused to let students catch up with him.

Mark jumped into the void. "Or," he said, and then stopped right there for a few seconds.

Penelope said, "Or?"

Anton said, "Or what?"

Mark said, "Or, one week from today, you should arrive with thirteen copies of five hundred words of engaging, original, pitch-perfect, chosen prose about a wise old homeless woman who lives with her piano-playing cat on Neptune and wakes to an alarm clock ringing in the dawn of a new day. Go away now, and just write something the rest of us need to read."

Had he yelled Fire!, he wouldn't have cleared the room as quickly.

FIVE

1.

Before he left the classroom on Wednesday, Mark got an email with a last-minute invite to a poetry slam from two students in last fall's class, and he replied with regrets and an excuse about another commitment, a lie he regretted before he was halfway across campus. Near Hum Hall, he crossed paths with Althea Morgan and Rita Jebdi, who asked him to join them for a drink at a new tapas bar in town, which assuaged his guilt about lying to the former students, even though he dodged the drink with a mention of the poetry slam and a quick glance at his watch. Was this bad behavior? Did his high hopes for getting a lot done over the long holiday weekend count as a reasonable excuse? Should he have accepted one or the other of the invitations?

These were the sort of questions that would plague Mark. For Paul, they were softballs, which he would answer happily and definitively, reliably hitting them out of the park. Student-poetry slam? No—devote some time to your own work. Drinks? No—two beers and you'll end up as chair of the department next year. No, no—no to both, but maybe we should try that tapas bar some night next week?

Are you tired? Did you see that article in the *Times*? Should we do laundry this weekend? There was a limit to how long Mark felt like Mark without answering and asking such questions. Paul's five-month stint away was too long, and the resumption of email and telephone contact, which still hadn't happened, wouldn't rectify the situation, and neither would a week together in Rome during spring break, which did not seem more plausible the longer Mark was without an airline reservation and Paul was just about everywhere in Europe but in Rome. Paul hadn't slipped away just yet, and neither had he, but Mark recognized the early warning signs—his fading interest in social life, the instinct to elude prolonged exposure to other people. Only twelve human beings were exempt from his antisocial impulse. Mark didn't understand why he would have happily spent an hour talking about a revision or a few draft pages with Max or Dorothy or even Jane before he left campus, but he was not so far gone—not yet—that he felt he could say this to Althea and Rita, or to the friends whose emailed invitations to dinners, lectures, and movies he had turned down.

Despite his resolve to get started immediately on his own work in Ipswich, Mark headed to Cambridge, hoping that an overnight infusion of Paulness might set him back to rights. This seemed like a perfect plan until he met Dennis in the hallway outside Paul's apartment and neither of them could hear what the other was saying. Something loud was going on in the building, and though Mark didn't expect they'd find it any quieter in Paul's place, he led the way to the kitchen table because Dennis was barefoot, wearing only shiny blue sweatpants and no shirt, and Mark's initial concern that someone passing by would mistake their meeting for a romantic rendezvous was getting mixed up with the noise and turning into something that felt suspiciously like hope.

Seated across from each other at the table, it was possible to shout and be heard. Dennis was having all of the floors in his vast home refinished "for the baby," or maybe he'd said, "before D-Day." His wife was staying with her mother through the weekend. Dennis had found a crew of guys from Vietnam who were willing to work at night, so he'd booked a room at the

Charles Hotel, and why didn't Mark have dinner with him there? Or Mark could stay there, too, and they could get those guys to refinish all of Paul's floors as a surprise.

The screeching and whirring suddenly stopped.

"Smoke break," Dennis said. "Another reason to trust those guys. They're up on the roof more than I am. They're doing all the floors in Allen's place next door, too. That's why I wanted to talk to you. I have a sense he might be thinking about selling. This is your chance."

Mark didn't ask, For what? Like many of their friends and acquaintances, Dennis really believed that living together in one place was a practical dilemma Mark and Paul had been unable to resolve for thirty years. Dennis assured Mark that the connecting wall with Allen's apartment was not structural, and if Mark moved in with Paul—Allen had a corner unit—it would always just be the four of them on the top floor, forever.

Mark said, "Well, five, right?"

Dennis said, "You're counting the baby?"

Mark stood up. "I'm on my way to Ipswich."

Dennis said, "Have you been to that new Mexican place in the Square?"

Mark walked to the refrigerator and poked his head inside for a minute. "You don't want an old pork tenderloin, do you? Or a shirt?" Dennis was distractingly handsome, and disarmingly indiscriminate. Mark wanted him to leave now, not to eliminate the temptation he represented but to spare Mark the disappointment he knew he would feel if he admitted to Dennis and himself that he was never going to take off his shirt. He didn't consider it a virtue, his monogamy, and he sometimes envied and even admired adults who could manage multiple intimacies. But whenever he stumbled into the opening passage of a little love affair or a sex scene, he saw the end of the story, saw himself more dazed than delighted, more alone than he could tolerate. This was just another of his limits.

"Couldn't you go for some nachos? I've also been craving tacos—you know, the old-fashioned crispy-shell ones? One of us should have married a Mexican." Dennis leaned way back in his chair and stared at the ceiling for a while, maybe to show off his torso, maybe to think through the logistics of acquiring a young bride from south of the border. "I have to admit I don't like frozen margaritas. I don't get the whole crushed-ice thing. It's hard to beat straight-up tequila."

One aspect of casual sex Mark didn't miss was this sort of conversation after the fact, when it became clear whom the other guy thought he was with.

A door slammed above them. "Their break's over already?" Dennis stood up. "I should've jumped into the shower while they were gone."

Now, though, he'd have an audience.

Dennis paused at the front door. "You will mention the place next door to Paul?"

"I will," Mark said. And it occurred to him that maybe he'd overestimated his own role in Dennis's story, that all Dennis ever wanted from him was casual conversation. "Thanks for thinking of him."

"I was thinking of all of us."

"All five," Mark said, but it was lost to the screeching of the sanders.

Mark cleared out the refrigerator and made a couple of round trips through Paul's place. The floorboards in the hall and near the windows were dinged up and dull. He checked the closets for no good reason, though he did snag another one of Paul's ancient flannel shirts and stuffed it into his bag. He knew if he circled around the rooms a few more times he would spend the next week on his knees with a rented sander and two gallons of polyurethane, so he shut off the lights.

While he let the Saab warm up, he checked his phone. He already had four revisions from students to add to the pile he'd accumulated this week, and Sharon had blind-copied him into an email she'd written to Paul's colleagues in Boston about her first few days with the refugees on Lesbos and news that Paul's boat would finally be docking next Wednesday or Thursday, and she hoped they could meet before she flew home. When he got to Ipswich, Mark found a postcard from his great friend Rachel Reed. She had retired from McClintock College last summer, and she was visiting a new grandson in Denver. Rachel detailed all of the delights of her son, the new grandkid, the Rockies in distance, and then wrote, "All of this, all of this, and still I miss the teaching. What is the matter with me? And who else could I tell?" This made Mark wish she were in town. Rachel was one of the only people who would have understood that he wanted to have dinner with her and wasn't going to.

Before he went to bed on Wednesday night, Mark had two more revisions of Technical Exercises, a draft of a second, even longer op-ed from the Professor, along with the looming threat of those sixty-five pages of his novel, and more student revisions surely on the way over the long weekend, and what with seven days of alternating sleet and snow and pounding rain, and the old pork loin, which didn't smell deadly and tasted just fine swimming in lemon and capers and cream, Mark didn't leave the house for a week, and just about an hour before he packed up his bag late on Wednesday morning, a long-threatened blizzard had clobbered Cape Cod and then unexpectedly veered due east out over the Atlantic, so it was clear sailing all the way to campus.

2.

Dorothy, Jane, Julio, Rashid, and Willa were lined up in alphabetical order beside Mark's office when he arrived just before one o'clock. As he unlocked his door, Mark said, "Where's everybody else?"

"Actually, Max and Anton were here a minute ago," Dorothy said.

"Not before me," Jane said.

"Wasn't Willa here first?" Rashid said.

The brim of Willa's cowboy hat was tipped up. She was studying something on the ceiling.

Julio waved his hand, and everyone turned to see Leo at the top of the staircase, heading their way with a little terrier on a leash. Julio yelled, "Take a ticket," leaned back in his puffy parka, and slid down the wall to sit. One of his ears was plugged into something amusing.

"Oh, great," Dorothy said. "The stress pets are back."

"For midterms," said Rashid.

"I feel calmer already," Leo said. "He's Welsh."

"I did make an appointment," Jane said.

She did—for one forty-five, but Mark knew saying so would only give the others another reason to consign her to the doghouse. "Three things," he said.

Julio said, "What's his name?"

Dorothy said, "Yappy."

Leo said, "Punter."

Dorothy said, "Fleabag."

Mark swung open the door and let it bang against the wall, which drew everyone's attention, including the dog's. "For starters, I have comments on revisions for Dorothy, Julio, Rashid, Leo, and Willa, which you can read while you wait, or you can take them away and we'll talk after class about any questions or confusions you want to clear up. If Max and Anton show up again, someone can tell them to knock and pick up their comments, as well. Second, might someone want to leave and come back at, say, one forty-five or two?" He dropped his bag to the floor and pulled out a folder.

The dog yapped.

"If it makes such a big difference," Jane said, buttoning her cape, avoiding Mark's gaze, "I can come back."

"Perfect. Thanks, Jane."

Julio said, "You said there were three things."

Mark said, "Thirdly, Leo—No."

"Just for today?"

Mark said, "Not a chance."

Leo knelt beside Punter and pulled him against his thigh, as if the dog were under assault. "He's sensitive to rejection."

"I checked," Mark said. "He never registered for the course." He pulled Leo's revisions from his folder. "The new version of the hit-and-run is really effective. Well done. Now, take these notes and find some place to ditch the dog before class."

While Mark was shuffling through his pile and doling out his comments on the revisions, Max returned. "Are you having a yard sale?"

"You are, finally, in this new draft." Mark handed Max two pages. "At last, we see the money change hands in this revision. We can talk later or after class."

"Okay, but just one thing—cradling the clarinet?" Max smiled. "Too much?"

Mark said, "I like that verb for the story, but I'm not sure how one cradles a skinny woodwind."

"Agreed," said Max. "I'll catch you later."

Dorothy and Rashid wandered down the hall, shoulder to shoulder, reading their comments, trailed by Leo and his foster dog.

Willa hadn't moved. Staring up at an acoustic tile, she said, "Go ahead, Julio. I'd rather wait a few minutes."

Julio stood up. "I could come back. I didn't eat lunch yet."

Willa didn't say anything.

Mark nodded, and Julio followed him into the office, closed the door, and sat down.

Julio whispered, "Is she all right?"

"She has an exam coming up," Mark said, which would surely be true eventually, though it didn't account for her indoor stargazing.

"I can relate," Julio said.

"I can't save you from Statistics, and I'm not serving hot lunch," Mark said, "so what can I do for you?"

"Guarantee I'm getting at least a B+ in this class?"

"If you keep submitting drafts on time of the same quality, and eventually revise at least one of the Technical Exercises and both short stories," Mark said, as he paged through his grade book, "I don't see why you wouldn't be on target for a C."

"I'm a senior." This wasn't a complaint. It was more of a gentle reminder.

Mark said, "Congratulations."

Julio said, "Would you mind checking that grade again? My phone has a calculator, if you want to borrow it."

"It's pretty simple math," Mark said. "Thirteen multisyllabic words on the first Technical Exercise—"

"Okay, but that won't count," Julio said, suddenly very upright in the chair. "I'm not revising that one for the portfolio."

"Unless I missed it here," Mark said, squinting at his page of notes, "I don't see any revision of the hit-and-run story. That's the one in which you wrote that fantastically long comma splice."

"I get it. Conjunctions," he said, and then added, "I've been using tons of them lately. And everybody loved my tag sale. That should bring me up to around a B, I think."

Mark flipped a few pages in his notebook. "I'm just looking for when I saw a revision of that story."

"You didn't give us a deadline for revisions, and I've done everything else on time." His voice was getting louder, and he must've been sweating because he ripped off his parka and stuffed it down behind him in the chair. "And I did say some things in class."

"During the first week or two," Mark said, "and then I'd say you let other people do most of the heavy lifting. Or am I remembering our time in class incorrectly?"

Julio didn't say anything.

Mark said, "That was a genuine question."

Julio said, "I just didn't think participation would really end up counting for so much."

"And punctuation and syntax," Mark said. "And revisions."

"I get all that," Julio said. "You could remind us about the participation, though."

Mark nodded. "Remind me, Julio. What year do you graduate?"

"Soon, with your cooperation," he said. Finally, he smiled. "I'm not blowing off this class. It's my favorite, really, but I sometimes don't have much to say about the stories. I mean, usually I just like them."

"That's not because you're reading each of them twice and writing down lots of notes in the margins before the workshops," Mark said.

"True," Julio said. He was shaking his head, lips pursed. Eventually, he pulled on his parka. "I really thought talking to you was going to put me in a good mood."

Mark said, "You're better than what you've done so far."

"Room for improvement," Julio whispered. "Story of my life." He had gone all soft suddenly, slumping in the chair, hands folded at his waist.

Was he feeling defeated, or was this a show of self-pity? Impossible to tell. Did he want empathy or sympathy or a B+? Not clear. But he was a senior who had yet to demonstrate a mastery of commas and conjunctions, so Mark said, "When should I expect the first revision?"

"Tomorrow," Julio said, and then winced, as if he'd instantly realized he could have gotten away with a promise of next week.

"Great. I'll be here, and eager to read."

Julio nodded and didn't say anything else on his way out.

Willa walked in and tossed her hat onto the little desk under the window. "What a waste of time meditating is," she said. She took off her long coat and folded it in half so it would fit beside her hat. She was wearing cowboy boots and a flowery short-sleeved sheath dress last seen on an episode of *Little House on the Prairie*, and she was wishing she had dropped Abnormal Psychology, wishing the professor would stop using the term *self-experiments*, which was an oxymoron, and wondering if her revision of the tag sale story now started in medias res—"in the middle of things," she added, in case Mark didn't have as much Latin as she did. She handed Mark his annotated version of her revision.

"Yes and no," Mark said, looking over his comments. "You've done great work to get the tag sale up and running, but if the story opened with her feverishly sorting through stuff as she does in the fourth line—would much be lost?"

"No." Willa was still clomping around behind him. "Only the stuff about the weather, but why shouldn't the rain just happen, right?"

Mark said, "There is a lot of meteorological buildup."

Willa sat down. "Why don't you teach a course in Shakespeare?"

Mark didn't say anything.

Willa said, "I'm about to graduate and—in our class lately, I've been seeing what an idiot I am. I mean, I see how I'm trying to write some profound story, but I've never even read a whole play by Shakespeare. Not even in high school."

Mark said, "Didn't you have to read *Romeo and Juliet*?"

Willa scrubbed her short hair as if she were in a shower. It actually looked better in the aftermath. "CliffsNotes and fast-forwarding through the old movie version. How can I graduate college without ever reading a single play by the greatest writer in the history of the world?" She was a remarkably attentive student, a writer who took reader responses to heart, a little harsh as a critic, and a terrible judge of what to put on before she left the house. She was on her way to becoming a surgeon, and something—maybe a comment made by her high school English teacher years ago, maybe the creative-writing class, maybe the ersatz form of meditation she'd been practicing in the hall—had put Shakespeare in her way.

"Lucky you," Mark said. "I envy you the chance to read the plays for the first time as an adult. You are in for a treat. Why don't you start with *Romeo and Juliet*?"

"Now?"

It was obviously a genuine question. "During spring break? We could meet when you get back to talk about what you made of it."

"And then another play maybe?"

Mark said, "He wrote a few."

"For credit?" Willa looked hopeful. "Is it too late to make it an official Independent Study with a grade?" She was pre-med, and she had already learned that being a doctor meant getting the credit.

A knock at the door brought Willa to her feet. When she opened the door, she said, "Oh." She left Charles in the hall and collected her hat and coat. "Thank you for everything, Mark," she said, staring down Charles.

Mark stood up. Charles didn't move, though he did raise his eyebrows when Willa put on her cowboy hat. Mark glanced back at Willa. She was texting something. Charles looked up at the ceiling to relieve his exasperation. Willa moved to the doorway, turned her back to Charles as she poked at her phone. Charles ahemmed twice.

It wasn't Shakespeare, but it was a compelling little drama.

Willa said, "I'm off." She blew past Charles without a word.

"Can I just ask you a question?" Charles seemed unsure about entering a room formerly occupied by Willa.

Mark saw Jane's red hood rising up the staircase, and he knew she was capable of bargaining her way in before Charles and possibly scaring him off entirely, so he hurried Charles inside, closed the door, sat at his desk, and swiveled toward Charles. Had he always been Charles? He was an awkward guy, with a lot of him bubbling up against the seams of the pale blue button-down shirts and chinos he wore every day. And his beard was still looking like a parched and patchy lawn. It was easy to imagine Charles was in transition, but it was not so easy to know which way he was headed.

Charles didn't sit. He grabbed the back of the alumni chair and leaned forward. "I'm trying to figure out how to write my story in Russian but make it English."

Mark said, "Is it set in Russia?"

"Italy," Charles said.

Mark said, "Do you speak Russian?"

"No," Charles said, "but they do."

"The Italians?"

This occasioned a thoughtful pause. "Some of them are going to have to, I guess."

Mark said, "Who's telling the story, Charles?"

"I see what you mean," he said. His hands had gone beet red against the black chair.

Although Mark had no idea what either of them meant by anything they'd said so far, something about Charles's serious demeanor made him think the conversation might yet pay off, so he tossed another ruble into the pot. "If you had to name the genre—I mean, thriller, caper, mystery—"

"Oh, it's a love story," Charles said. "Unrequited."

That was a relief. "One way to handle foreign languages in English prose is to have the narration establish the speaker's language and then give the speech in English. Or, you can use indirect free discourse as you did in the tag sale story, letting us hear the tone and quality of the character's voice through the narration. And you can drop in a few italicized words in the speaker's native tongue—simple words that readers can interpret by context without translation."

Charles stood up straight. "Hello and goodbye."

Mark said, "Thank you."

Charles said, "*Grazie.*"

Mark said, "*Spasibo.*"

Charles didn't like the sound of that one. "So I should warn you—in the draft page for class, I didn't really do such a good job with the languages."

"That's why you write a draft and give it to readers. It feels like a risk, but it always pays off."

"No offense, but I'm supposed to meet with Professor Arsenault about my Senior Project for Sociology soon. We're having a problem with the cross-country team and some other jocks signing out all the anxiety dogs and running around with them in Breakheart Reservation all day, so there are no dogs left for the kids who need them."

Mark said, "We can talk again about the draft pages after your workshop."

"Page," Charles said. "But now you've got me thinking about how dogs understand what you say, no matter what language it's in."

Mark said, "I think Jane might be waiting to see me. Good luck with the dogs."

Charles said, "They're just innocent bystanders," and told Jane to go in as he passed her.

Jane had evidently spent her time in the hall rearranging the contents of six bulging folders, which she stacked up on Mark's desk, and then left to retrieve her satchel and cape. "I know you are extremely busy," she said, shoving Mark's bag to the far side of his desk to make room for her knapsack. "It's that time of year. Everyone is," she added, just to be sure she hadn't let slip an inadvertent compliment. "I don't want to put the blame on anyone in particular, but I am pretty worried about my story draft and how hard some people are going to come down on me." She sat. "And if we have some extra time, I want to talk about those dates we had to pick for our story workshops because there are a lot more blank spaces than stories after spring break, and I don't understand how you expect us to fill them all up." She seemed annoyed that she hadn't yet had to speak over Mark. "I was thinking about how you could maybe coach the other kids to see things from my point of view once in a while."

Mark said, "Have you ever read *Romeo and Juliet*?" He was thinking about Willa, and Shakespeare, and Charles leaning on the back of the chair as if it were the railing of a balcony. It was not yet a coherent thought, and he could see that Jane was confused.

"Me?"

Mark nodded.

"A long time ago."

"What is it Juliet says in the balcony scene?"

Jane looked amused, or maybe worried? "Is this about *Wherefore art thou*?"

"That's it," Mark said. "It's one of dozens of questions in her speeches. And Romeo, his speech is full of questions, too. If you look at the text, you'll be amazed by how many questions they pose to each other."

Jane didn't say anything.

Mark said, "You could say that questions are the language of love. They invite someone else into the conversation, into the story."

Jane said, "I thought we weren't allowed to ask questions during our workshops."

This was not going well. Mark had hoped he could help Jane alter her declamatory style in class discussions by translating her comments into questions. She wasn't having it. "Don't worry about the open spaces after spring break on the schedule," he said. "Everyone has to bring at least one revision to the class of every story that is going into the final portfolio."

Jane was transcribing this into a notebook. She looked relieved. Finally, Mark had come up with something she could sink her teeth into.

"We can bring revisions to the class more than once?"

Mark said, "Absolutely."

Jane nodded her approval. "So, choosing early workshop dates leaves me more time for revising with you and then the whole class."

Mark said, "Was that a question?"

"Oh, no. I'm just thinking out loud."

Mark said, "I was wondering how you feel about waiting till Thursday to have your workshop?" He knew it was hopeless, but he was still clinging to that balcony. "It might be useful to watch and see how a few other stories are treated today before you are on the receiving end. Does that make sense?"

Jane looked intrigued. "The Thursday stories—are you going to force everybody to read them at home before class tomorrow?"

She had mastered the form, if not the spirit of the question. "That's the idea," he said.

"Then I don't mind," Jane said. She leaned over and extracted a folder from her pile on Mark's desk, filed away the notes she'd taken, packed the folders into her bag, and donned her cape. She checked the time on her phone. "I usually like getting here first, but there's something nice about not having people knocking on the door while we're trying to talk."

Just thinking aloud. Mark said, "I'll see you in ten minutes."

"Twelve," Jane said, and she closed the door on her way out.

3.

The first fifteen minutes of class were devoted to raffling off the workshop dates for the rest of the semester, which inevitably gave way to questions about submitting revisions, exactly what had to be in the final portfolio, and requests for a review of the percentage breakdown of the grade value of everything until the Professor lost patience with the administrative details and said, "We have work to do. Today, for the only time until the last class of the semester, we will ask the writer to read her or his work aloud as we annotate our printed copies. At this point, our aim is to give brief responses to illuminate for the writer what we understand, what we expect, and anything incomprehensible in the literal text of the story's opening page or two. Briefly."

The Professor had so little patience for the time it took each writer to read a page or two that he had tried every semester to persuade Mark to let him speed-read the drafts aloud, but Mark was committed to giving the students the stage. So, as soon as the last word of the first draft page was intoned, the Professor yelled, "What is at stake? Charles? Charles!" That woke everyone up. And after the stakes were identified by Charles, with assistance from Dorothy! Leo! and Willa!, a few students—Julio! Rashid! Jane!— speculated on the arcs for the main characters, and then the Professor asked Virginia! Anton! Max!—and keep it brief, Max—about opportunities they hoped to see exploited later in the story, and then elicited a series of literal confusions, starting with Rashid! Finally, he slapped the draft on the desk and held up another.

This was the Professor's interpretation of the Socratic method. It fell to Mark to temper the performance with a Platonic question or two.

"I've got Penelope in my sights," the Professor said.

When Mark looked around the room, twelve familiar faces stared from the windowsills at the twelve writers at the table. He said, "Would you like to read us what you wrote, Penelope?"

And but for the occasional *Julio? Virginia? Jane?* from Mark, requesting a clarification or an example, so it went for more than an hour.

When he had first agreed to design the course with the Professor, Mark had assumed that students would always read their stories aloud to the workshop, as was true in every creative-writing class he'd ever taken or observed or even heard about. The listeners in those classes were not given printed copies of the stories in advance—typically, they didn't even have printed copies to consult while the stories were being read aloud in class—so they never wrote responses but simply spoke about what had just been read while the writer listened. Mark had explained all of this to the Professor.

So we wouldn't have to teach them anything, the Professor had said.

Mark had said, *Ask anyone.* Not a persuasive counterargument, he knew, but he hadn't anticipated any resistance.

The Professor had said maybe they should go away and think about it all for a week, but he did concede that what Mark was proposing sounded sort of appealing, really fun, too, and it would definitely make for a terrific little story-time program in a nursery school.

4.

No one stayed after class on Wednesday, though there were several shouted threats about emailed revisions on their way. And on Thursday, Julio was waiting for Mark at his office door with one revision of his own, and three from others who hadn't wanted to wait in line, which he delivered before speeding away, promising to return on Monday with more. Leo had evidently stopped by, as well. Taped to Mark's office door was an 8x10 color portrait of Punter, the Welsh terrier, with a caption: *Why can't we be friends?*

Dorothy, Max, and Virginia dropped by with questions about a word or phrase in one of the stories they'd each revised four or five times already. Isaac turned up with new iterations of all three of his Technical Exercises, though he really wanted to give Mark a play-by-play of the curling club's first victory because they'd stunned the club team from Wesleyan, and Isaac had been wait-listed there.

On his way to class, Mark spotted something red huddling by the door of the Arts Building. As he approached, Jane waved.

"Hello, Professor."

Mark almost made a joke about her addressing him by his title, but Jane looked a little pale. And he was her professor.

"I hope you don't mind," Jane said, rushing ahead to hold open the door, "but I thought it would help if I walked in with you today. I could use some backup."

Mark said, "My prediction? You're going to be surprised."

Jane said, "You're just like me—a born optimist."

She didn't look at all surprised when the workshop for her story elicited several suggestions for exploring intriguing opportunities present in her first two pages, and she was smiling smugly when Dorothy posed a genuinely provocative question about the last paragraph, which Jane acknowledged with an enthusiastic, "Great minds think alike!"

The Professor reminded Jane that she wasn't here during her workshop. But Mark knew she was.

The Professor poked and prodded them through the opening pages of the remaining stories, forcing everyone to say something about each one, and as the last confusion was articulated about the last page of the last of the drafts, he said, "Pens, please."

Mark returned the confused gazes he was getting.

"This is by way of example, not as a required assignment," the Professor said. "However, if you are not able to bring your story draft to completion successfully, you may choose to write this 1,500-word Technical Exercise instead."

Anton said, "Should we write it down if we know we want to write our own story?"

Mark nodded. He was as surprised as everyone else that the Professor had decided to offer this option, after all. "I think you'll see that the details of the assignment will give you a clearer idea about starting in the middle of things, and how to create a rich backstory for your characters without compromising the forward momentum of your narration—"

"Wait a minute." This was Leo. "Should we be writing already?"

Max said, "Wild guess: yes."

Charles said, "Could you start again, then?"

Mark did, and added, "You'll also see what we mean by using a subplot to comment on the central conflict."

Dorothy said, "Scenario?"

"The central character is Ellen, a twenty-year-old woman who works as a waitress in a diner," the Professor said. "Ellen did not grow up in the town where she works. She moved from her hometown when she was in high school and became pregnant. Today, for the first time, Ellen leaves her five-year-old child home alone while she goes to work."

"Five?" Rashid had done the math. "So she was—"

"Yes," the Professor said. "The child instantly and efficiently establishes that history, right? The story must be set in an identifiable time period prior to 1970."

"No cell phones," Leo said.

"No *Roe v. Wade*," Dorothy said.

Penelope said, "No computers, really. Certainly not home models, right?"

"No way," Julio said.

The Professor said, "The real time of the story is mostly Ellen's workday—she enters the diner in advance of its 6:00 a.m. opening, and her shift ends at 4:00 p.m. At some point, Ellen must wait on someone, or a group of customers, that she knew before she left her hometown. The story ends as Ellen approaches her home and sees that her front door is open."

Charles said, "She can't go inside?"

"No."

"So her kid is gone?" This was Julio again.

"Wild guess number two," said Max. "Readers should know what happened by virtue of what happens up to that moment."

Rashid said, "Technical Limits?"

The Professor said, "No more than 1,500 words. Third-person, limited to Ellen. Past tense. And—"

"We're not done?" Virginia was speaking for a lot of the others.

Somebody thanked god that this was optional and not required.

"The following suggestive elements must appear in the story," the Professor said. "First, when Ellen arrives, she sees a dog tied up in front of the diner. The dog is there when she leaves to go home. Second, the front wall of the diner is a transparent, plate-glass window. Third, above the booths at the rear of the diner, the wall is mirrored glass—so Ellen can see what she looks like, often must encounter her own reflection."

Max said, "You did say fifteen million words, right? The scenario is at least a thousand."

"Oh, I get it," Willa said, "the dog—why is he there, all alone? will he be all right?—is basically the kid she left at home."

"Thus, a subplot," said Max.

Mark nodded. "And," he said.

"Oh, come on." Julio dramatically laid down his pen. "There's more?"

"Bear in mind," Mark said, "this is a story about a working woman. The details of her habits, routines, demeanor, and conversation at work have to be convincing and illuminating."

Max said, "Action."

Rashid said, "Is."

Dorothy said, "Character."

"Couldn't have said it better myself," Mark said.

The Professor said, "Now, go away."

5.

Penelope didn't stand up with the others, and Anton was jiggling nervously near the classroom door. When everyone else was gone, Anton said, "Are you going back to your office, Mark?"

He wasn't, but he was now. "I am," he said.

"I can wait," Penelope said.

"I can't," Anton said, and shot out into the hall.

Mark said, "I got the revisions you sent, Penelope, and I'll have them done for Monday."

"I have classes before and after this one, so I haven't been able to meet with you sooner, but my physics class isn't meeting on Monday, so—"

"So it's a date," Mark said. When she smiled, she looked more Asian than Andean, but her voice seemed to be inflected with some other part of the globe Mark could not identify. "Anything you want me to be thinking about besides the revisions and your story draft?"

"Do you remember Nina? Nina Maranapatha?"

"That Nina is a good egg," Mark said. "And a really elegant writer."

Penelope nodded enthusiastically. "She's the one who told me to take this class. We're doing a joint thesis. You know about crypto-currencies, right?"

Mark said, "Bitcoin?"

"Exactly." Penelope opened the flap of her satchel, held it near the table, and as she swept in her jumble of draft pages and notes she explained that she and Nina were trying to work out adaptive algorithms to resolve stability issues associated with crypto-currency revaluations.

Mark said. "We've just hit the limit of my understanding of crypto-currencies." In truth, his limit was the word *Bitcoin*.

Penelope laughed, and as she headed out the door, she said, "They are sort of like black holes, aren't they?" Another area of the universe in which Penelope was surely light-years beyond him.

Anton was waiting for Mark at the entrance to Hum Hall, shiny red car coat in hand. They climbed up to the third floor in silence, and when Mark unlocked his office door, he heard Anton huffing and puffing, trying to catch his breath. They took to their respective chairs, and Anton leaned over and dropped his coat in the corner.

"I don't have anywhere else to hide it," he said when he was upright again. "Do you mind?"

He *was* wearing flannel-lined jeans and a wool turtleneck sweater. "What else can I do for you?"

"You're going to get a letter from Dean Braxton," he said. "Unless you already did?"

"I haven't looked at my email since noon," Mark said. "Do you want me to check now?"

Anton shook his head dismissively. "It's about me missing classes. You're also getting something from one of the doctors, but it doesn't tell you anything you don't know. They don't think this new drug is working. Tomorrow, I'm having a bunch of new scans and tests, and then something on Monday that will take all day. That's why I had to run out of class today. I didn't want to say so in front of Penelope, but I've been drinking this stuff every three hours that makes me—it goes through you."

"I'm amazed you made it through class."

"Not quite," Anton said. "Sorry for the gory details."

Mark said, "I'm really sorry you have to live through this."

"We'll see," Anton said. His breathing was still labored.

"I want to see you live through this, Anton, hard as it must be."

"I just want to finish our class, Mark, that's all, really and—oh, boy." He bowed his head. His shoulders shook. And for a few long moments, he wept, occasionally raising his arms and holding his hands palm-out toward Mark. To apologize? To warn him to stay away? Eventually, he wiped his hands across his face, sat up straight. "Talking to you always does this."

"I blame that stuff you've been drinking," Mark said.

"And I can't eat anything till tomorrow night," Anton said, smiling, "so that might be putting me in a bad mood, too. If I don't make it to class on Monday, I'll bring my comments about the stories on Wednesday."

"That'll work well this time," Mark said, "because the first four writers are emailing their stories on Saturday, and we'll all print our own copies so we can read them in advance."

"But after that, we all print thirteen copies and bring them to the class before our workshop, right?"

"Exactly," Mark said. These inane details mattered only to thirteen people in the world, but the work of inventing them, negotiating them, valuing them, remembering them, confirming them, supporting them, and occasionally propping them up meant they were worth something more than the paper syllabus on which they had been printed. They became the crypto-currency for the classroom, the basis for the transactions that bound them each to the other.

Anton had pulled out his notebook, and he was flipping around, looking for something. "I know I wrote it down," he said.

Mark guessed Anton was looking for something Max had said in class, a smart and very kind suggestion. Max had said he saw an opportunity in Anton's story, which opened near the end of a high school cross-country race when the young man in the lead inexplicably collapses and his nemesis and classmate stops to help him, apparently sacrificing his chance at a college scholarship. The clear implication, which was evident to everyone in the class, was that the young man who fell would die by the story's end. Max suggested that it might be interesting to have a time break and take up the story a year later, when we could learn that the young man hadn't died, and the other guy was living with the consequences of having given up his chance for that scholarship. Twice, over objections from other readers about the clear suggestion of a mortal illness, Max had said, "He doesn't have to die."

"Would it be okay if we talked about this next Wednesday? I'll find it by then." Anton slapped his notebook shut. "My cousin is coming by soon to drive me home."

"That'll work," Mark said. "Your story isn't due till after spring break."

"That Monday, right? For a workshop on Wednesday?"

Mark nodded. "And as long as you're going to be lying around all weekend, eating home-cooked meals," Mark said, "you might want to find some way to turn that nephew in your tag sale story into the buyer's son, as Rashid suggested."

Anton stood up. "I've been making a list of suggestive words that might help, too," he said, glancing at the coat in the corner.

Mark stood and opened the door. "Might I suggest you find that scarf again?"

Anton said, "You didn't think that was a little too—French, or something?"

"It's not a beret," Mark said. "And it's supposed to snow on Friday."

Anton pushed the alumni chair back, grabbed his coat off the floor, and pulled the long blue and yellow scarf from one of the arms. "Ta-da." He wound it around his neck. "I hope you're happy," he said as he slipped past Mark into the hall. He stopped, turned, and waved.

Mark said, "I'll look for you on Wednesday."

"I know," Anton said.

SIX

1.

Mark treated all good news on the literary front as a surprise attack, so instead of celebrating or bragging like a normal person on Friday morning when the *New York Times* accepted his latest op-ed for publication, he put on a beanie and retreated to the porch with his laptop to review the editor's notes and reread what he had written. He didn't hate his prose, and most of the editor's questions and suggestions made sense to him, but when he got to the very end—*Professor Mark Sternum teaches creative writing at Hellman College. He is the author of*—he experienced that peculiar confusion that crept over him when he dreamed he had turned up in the classroom naked. He didn't enjoy exposing his ambitions, and the beanie wasn't much help in covering up his shortcomings.

Mark tried to rouse the Professor, but it was no use. The Professor was not on call. He did not exist on an as-needed basis. In fact, he was the repository of everything unnecessary that mattered to Mark, which is why the Professor reliably came to life only in the classroom, that kingdom of the inessential, temple of the discretionary, home of the elective.

The Professor was a fiction, and Creative Writing was unimaginable without him.

Who but the entirely superfluous Professor Mark had invented could sermonize with a straight face about syntax and grammar and spelling while the president of the United States tweeted about "unpresidented acts" and his Department of Education tweeted out a misspelling of the name of W.E.B. Du Bois and followed up with "our deepest apologizes for the earlier typo"? Who but this profligate Professor would spend his time typing a 400- or 500-word response to every 250 words of narrative prose every student wrote every week of the semester? Mark would have quit his job if he'd had to anticipate writing the 50,000 words of criticism the Professor produced for each class, when a few check marks and exclamation points penned into the margin of a student story were all that was required. So if the prolix Professor's peculiar habit of treating original prose so seriously also inspired him to write a book every two or three years and some incidental essays to support it, Mark was willing to act as factotum, editing those manuscripts into shape and accepting invitations to read or talk about the published work. It was the least he could do.

Fortunately, Mark actually enjoyed the tedium of the editorial work assigned to him and soon was absorbed by the challenge of trying to intuit the logic behind the copyeditor's preferences in punctuation and syntax, and attempting to negotiate compromises, even though the *New York Times* manual of style proved to be about as flexible as the Professor. He signed off on a near-to-final draft of the op-ed on Friday evening, and before he shut his laptop he found an email from Dean Braxton, who wanted to meet mid-morning on Monday in his office to talk about Anton and "the two others in your class with materials on file with our office," a reference that genuinely mystified Mark.

Half an hour later, Mark was still rummaging in his cabinets, hoping to discover a hamburger and fries behind the cans of diced tomatoes and white beans, when he got an apologetic and slightly frantic call from Norman Chester. The venerable professor emeritus had just been informed that his capacious office on the ground floor of Hum Hall would be outfitted with two new IKEA desks and chairs over spring break to "more appropriately accommodate our adjunct colleagues" unless Chester identified a member of the full-time faculty who was willing to share his office.

"You can have the real desk," Chester said. "It's the Morris chair I don't want to lose, and with two of those kiddie desks, it would have to go."

There were also approximately eight hundred overdue library books stacked like the ruins of an abandoned pueblo, a century's worth of un-collected final exams in shirt boxes arranged by date on the bookshelves, Chester asleep in the Morris chair most afternoons, and photocopies of all sixty-three madly metronomic poems from *A Shropshire Lad* taped to the wall. Chester must have sensed that Mark was reviewing the inventory be-cause he apologized again for telephoning at dinnertime and offered to buy Mark lunch on Monday at noon at the café in the library. "That will give us both sufficient time to consider the ramifications of your sharing a space so deeply associated with me," he added, and then hung up.

Mark found a venerable slab of lasagna in the back of the freezer, and once he'd hacked away the ice crystals, it looked enough like food to merit a few minutes in the microwave. While it spun and sputtered, he also received eleven emails, a raft of pictures and videos, and a text from Paul promising to call "at some ungodly hour on Saturday morning." Mark texted back to let Paul know he was in Ipswich. No response. The microwave dinged. His dinner was thoroughly desiccated. He dumped that into the trash, made a big batch of popcorn with extra olive oil, and sensing the need for some-thing proteinaceous, he opened a beer, put on his beanie and a bathrobe, and headed to the porch for a picnic with Paul.

Paul was many things, but he was not a man of many words. He loved Mark. He missed Mark. He would soon be installed in his apartment in Rome again, where he would be based until the end of June. He correctly guessed that Mark would not be making the transatlantic trip for spring break. In Paul's photographs and videos, the Aegean Sea featured promi-nently, often singularly, and it was deeply blue. Which was how Mark felt when he finished his beer and went back upstairs to the kitchen.

To cheer himself up, he made dessert—another beer, two cigarettes, and the remnants of the morning's coffee. He scrolled through Paul's emails again, looking for and then inventing something unexpected, something out of the blue, something that would qualify as the cherry on top. *I booked you a round-trip ticket to come to Rome for spring break! I bought Allen's apartment so you will move in with me once and for all! I'm coming home to spend spring break with you! I quit my stupid job!* In his imagination, Mark was a master of the plot twist, the surprise ending that seemed to solve everything but resolved nothing, the sort of deus ex machina students resorted to when they were dissatisfied with the inevitable consequences of the choices they had made, when they clearly saw their characters and did not love their limits.

A little before midnight, Dorothy, Max, and Rashid emailed their stories for Monday. Willa, Jane, and Julio had also sent revised Technical Exercises. And an editor at the *National Geographic* wanted to run his longer op-ed in its online edition after spring break. This was good news, but after some poking and prodding, Mark did see the underside. Soon, he would have no choice but to take up those sixty-five pages of his novel.

Some time after he went to bed—Mark couldn't tell if he'd been asleep for minutes or hours—something woke him. He slapped the pillows around and rolled over, searching for the source of the sound, but the ringing stopped before he landed on his phone. He sat up. He waited. The phone rang again, and this time he spotted the lit-up screen in the charger on a windowsill.

Mark said, "I'm here."

Paul said, "And here, dear man."

Mark said, "Where, exactly, are we?"

"Izmir," Paul said.

"It's all Greek to me," Mark said.

"Izmir's in Turkey," Paul said.

"I do get around," Mark said. He was trying to decide if it was a fading moon or a rising sun spilling light into his bedroom windows. "And as it is the job of the literary critic to state the obvious, I miss you."

Paul was leaving soon for a week in Sofia, and then a few days in Zagreb, and then he'd be back to Rome to set up a permanent office for the

Paean Project's ongoing work with refugees and to hire a regional director. He asked about Mark's work. Mark told him about this semester's students. He asked about Mark's writing. Mark told him some more about the students. He asked what Mark was writing.

Mark said, "Did you manage to see Sharon?"

Paul didn't say anything.

Mark finally delivered the news about the *Times*, immediately adding that "they're determined to run it on Wednesday," and then he tossed in the *National Geographic*. "They're demanding a lot of changes, so we'll see what they finally run of it."

"Bastards," Paul said. "They are constantly exploiting you. I bet they end up putting you on NPR again, and probably they'll even force you to do some TV. If you're not careful, they'll make another movie out of one of your books."

Mark didn't say anything.

"It's an accomplishment, not a public embarrassment or a crime," Paul said. "When were you going to tell me?"

Mark didn't say anything.

Paul said, "I end up feeling like a fool because I'm happy or proud of what you write."

"Sometimes the writing seems—I mean, compared to war and famine and cholera—it can seem sort of self-serving and petty. That's why I asked about Sharon. Because I want you to know that I am so confused and petty in your absence that I was annoyed she was going to see you and I wasn't."

Paul said, "I take that as a compliment." He had not seen Sharon, but he was confident she would join him in the Boston headquarters of the Paean Project this fall. He was hoping she would head up a public health initiative that was being redesigned to construe the city's homeless population not as vagrants and wastrels but as refugees.

"Now I feel even pettier," Mark said.

"My apartment in Rome is superb—tiny, but spectacular, with floor-to-ceiling windows overlooking the piazza. It's a little embarrassing," Paul said. "Does that help?"

Mark said, "Now, I'm so petty I envy you."

Paul was silent for a few long seconds. "Most of my time on that trawler was nothing but staring at the sea, but a few times we sighted a dinghy or dory stuffed with people. We'd signal them and lead them to a temporary camp on the coast that was prepared to receive them. There were bodies bandaged up with rags, kids crying. We'd wait offshore while they jumped in and waded to safety, such as it was. And do you know what I felt? I felt sorry for myself. Speaking of pettiness. I honestly felt sorry for myself, stuck on that trawler, a world away from you, drifting back out to sea instead of—"

Mark said, "It's been too long."

"We overshot our limits this time," Paul said. "Come to Italy when your semester ends. Save both of us."

"Okay," Mark said. It was now evident that the sun was rising. "When I get there, we are going to revise the syllabus for our lives."

"Okay," Paul said. "Right now, I have to catch a plane."

"Enjoy your peanuts," Mark said, "because that's definitely not on next semester's syllabus."

2.

At ten o'clock on Monday morning, the dean of students waved Mark into his office on the second floor of College Hall. The white brick building was identical to Hum Hall, but Nate Braxton's office was exactly twice as big as Mark's, and he didn't share it with anybody. "Thanks for coming, Mark. I promise not to keep you for long. I'm sure you're busy, too." Braxton paused to admire Mark's jeans and parka. "Wild weekend with the snow and rain. Impossible to know what to wear in this weather." He was wearing an elegant navy suit and a regimental-stripe tie, charcoal and pale blue, Hellman College colors. They'd met several times over the years, but all Mark really knew was that Braxton had a PhD in American History from Michigan or Wisconsin or one of the other great state universities in the Midwest. He assumed Braxton was one of the thousands of ambitious white guys in their thirties and forties who didn't get tenure after the federal government finally pried open the hiring and tenure process with diversity initiatives and so migrated into administrative positions where they implemented the federal guidelines that had cost them their academic careers. "Take a seat."

There were three high-back red-leather wing chairs facing the dean's vast desk, and four knockoff Chippendale chairs and a table under the window, evidently reserved for Braxton's gym bag and squash racquet. The dean pointed to the red chairs and sat at his desk. Mark sank half a foot into the soft leather seat, so he was forced to look up at Braxton, and the chair's wings obliterated his peripheral vision, so he was forced to look at nothing but Braxton.

Braxton opened a folder. "I want to let you know what's happening with a young man in your class."

"I know Anton," Mark said defensively.

Braxton said, "Terrible story."

"Able writer," Mark said, as if Anton's merits were being called into question, "and committed," he added.

"Good to hear," Braxton said. "That should make this easier."

Mark said, "Has something happened to Anton?"

"I think you know as much about his illness as I do, maybe more. Aside from the letter you saw, the doctors don't tell us anything. It's a privacy issue. I have met with his mother several times, and in recent weeks, she and the stepfather have come to think the commuting back from campus for treatments is taking a toll." Braxton closed his folder. "The student has finished the work to convert the two Incompletes he was carrying in his economics courses—or he's done enough to satisfy those faculty members."

Every apparently benign sentence Braxton uttered landed like a mallet on a peg, hammering Mark down deeper into that chair.

"Econ is his major, of course." Braxton pulled a printed form out of one of the desk drawers. "This writing class of yours is just an elective, right?"

"Yes," Mark said, "Anton elected to take it." He sensed he was being set up to persuade Anton to withdraw from the workshop, to convince him that he was not able to do the work required for a passing grade. Thus, the form Braxton had slid toward Mark.

"The mother is well aware of how much her son has enjoyed your class," Braxton said. "He speaks very highly of you."

"It feels odd to be speaking about Anton as if he's not here," Mark said.

"Well, he's not here." Braxton looked genuinely perplexed. "Or did you mean as if he already—as if he's no longer—"

"I just meant he is here, at the college, in the workshop, and he's twenty-one or twenty-two—an adult." Mark paused to stop his voice escalating into the counter-tenor range. "I think we ought to allow him to decide this."

Braxton said, "Decide what?" It was evidently a genuine question.

And a good one, as Mark had no ready answer.

Braxton said, "You want to consult the student about his final grade?" He flicked the form a few inches closer to Mark. "I'm just trying to get this kid a college degree. You give him a grade, and he's officially got his BA."

This was an unexpected twist, somehow both more generous and more manipulative than Mark's imagination of the dean's plot. Mark said, "I give him a grade today, and he's done?"

"Exactly," Braxton said.

Mark said, "Because he's sick?" This sounded more callous than he'd intended. Unfortunately, it also rang true to Mark, so he persisted. "What about the other two students you mentioned in your email?"

"If you haven't heard about accommodations for those students, it's because they decided not to declare their documented challenges or their need for special assistance."

Mark said, "But why not give them each a final grade right now?"

Braxton didn't say anything.

"Should we say automatic B+ for a missing limb? What's the grading curve for bilingual or trilingual students?"

Braxton slid the form back from the edge of his desk and stuck it into the file.

"Either they are our students or they're not," Mark said. "I don't think

I ought to have a hand in admissions, or who gets accommodations, or anything else. I'll happily take anyone who wins the registration lottery and gets a seat in the workshop. I'll take anyone you tell me is ours. But then I close the door." Mark knew his refusal to cooperate was mixed up with Anton's enthusiasm for the workshop, and his own affection for Anton, but that stew was also chock-full of headscarves and curling brooms and anxiety dogs and man buns and Red Riding Hood.

Braxton looked away. "This is not at all the conversation I anticipated," he said, and then he walked to the windows and stared out at his view of the muddy trails that looped around the pond and led out into the piney darkness of Breakheart Reservation.

Mark wanted to urge him to look for the ironworks, and sawmills, and the several centuries' worth of commercial enterprises that were no longer there, to listen for the chanting in the Common of demonstrators down the years demanding co-ed classrooms or protesting gender-neutral bathrooms, students picketing desegregation or race-based quotas, alumni decrying merit-based scholarships or need-blind admissions. Hellman had survived them all. Was it morally superior or more politically correct or more humane than the institutions and ethical debates it had outlasted? Yes and no, here and there, depending on where you stood. But whether from afar the college looked like the last bastion of elitism or the best breeding ground for a new social order really did not matter to Mark.

It had managed something unimaginable.

The college had preserved the classroom, that fragile home for possibility, that singular space devoted solely to potential, that venerable, evanescent moment in which we have the chance to see that there is more to us than anyone ever knew.

Braxton said, "With or without your help, we're going to find a way to make this happen." He ambled back to his desk and sat down. "Is there something I could say to change your mind, Mark?"

Mark said, "Anton hasn't completed even half of the work for his final portfolio."

Braxton narrowed his gaze, and his consternation slowly faded into disbelief.

Mark said, "Let me talk this over with Anton."

Braxton said, "The mother asked us to let her broach the topic with her son. I think we owe her that much, don't you?"

Mark didn't say no, but that was the truth. He also didn't feel he owed explanations to coaches for their star players being late to practice twice a week or a heads-up to helicopter parents who requested progress reports on their progeny. "I can imagine how insensitive or obstreperous or silly I seem, Nate."

"Add them all together and multiply by ten," Braxton said. "You do understand, I trust, that our conversation today was confidential."

"You mean I am not to say anything to Anton?"

"Honestly, I mean that I hope you will change your mind." He extracted that form from his folder, leaned over, and handed it to Mark. "Whatever the outcome, it will be decided before classes resume after spring break."

Mark said, "You can't assign a final grade for someone in my workshop."

Braxton said, "No, but until Friday, the student can withdraw without affecting his academic record." He stood and walked to the door. "I am confident we can find someone else in the department to accept what he's done as course credit for an Independent Study."

Mark said, "Why not give him a PhD while you're at it?" He paused at the door and said, "If the criterion is attitude, or pain and suffering, he's earned it."

3.

Mark was heading back to Hum Hall when he saw Althea Morgan waving from the far side of the pond. He knew he wouldn't respond well if the chair asked a favor or tried again to get him to consider taking over the reins of the department, so he veered onto a downhill path and went directly to the library. The reading room was full, a sure sign that midterms were not yet complete. With twenty minutes to squander before his lunch date with Norman Chester, Mark went to the end of the circulation desk and counted the number of students who had borrowed the story collections he'd put on reserve. Eight of the writers had signed out at least one of the books a total of thirty-one times, better numbers than he would have predicted.

The Professor refused to assign texts for the workshops, convinced that published work by established writers inspired imitation instead of innovation. And it was true that the few times Mark had brought in a story for everyone to read, students treated it as a kind of trump card, using its particular plot and prose style to praise or criticize stories written by their classmates. The reserve list was a compromise, and starting this week, after he printed out the Professor's typed responses to the first original stories, Mark typically attached photocopies of the contents page of each collection on reserve and checked off a few specific stories that he hoped might inspire or complicate each writer's revision process.

"Hey, Professor." A very tall young woman with an Afro and yellow-plastic eyeglasses was sidling toward him from her post at the checkout station. Lisa? Marina? Arlene? She'd been in a workshop two or three semesters ago, and she'd written a devastating story about a young man who was co-erced into giving his mother away at her second marriage to a man he feared.

Mark said, "I hope this job doesn't interfere with your writing."

"I'm taking a poetry workshop this semester," she said.

Regina? Lorna? "And?"

"I think I might have finally written a villanelle."

"Then you are way ahead of me," Mark said. "I just know enough to know that those are some intense limits to love."

"Well, I wouldn't exactly say I've fallen in love with poetry. Still in the flirting stage," she added, and dropped her gaze to the counter. "Would it be okay if I came by sometime to show you a story I wrote over Christmas?"

Mark said, "You know where to find me."

"I can make copies of those contents pages for you," she said. "Is that what you needed?"

Mark shook his head. "I can do that."

"It's sort of my job," she said. "I'll email them to you this afternoon."

"You're a champ." Cora? Bethany? He couldn't remember her name, but he would have liked to introduce her to the dean of students anyway. Wasn't everybody best served if she did her job, and Mark did his job, and the dean did his? "When you send the copies, send along that story you wrote. I've been searching for something to read over spring break."

"It's not quite—oh, never mind. You'll just tell me to let you read it, right?"

"Sounds like something I might say," Mark said, and he waved as he turned away. He was halfway down the corridor to the café when he heard someone repeatedly stage-whispering, "Professor? Professor?" The primary-color foam sofas lining the hallway were empty ahead of him, and he kept going until he heard, "Hey, Sternum!"

Norman Chester was attempting to hoist himself off a blue cushion that bent in half and snapped at his torso like a clamp every time he pressed down.

Mark hurried back and offered his hand.

Chester slapped away the offer. "No wonder none of these was occupied when I got here. Anyway, the café is overrun with undergraduates caffeinated to within an inch of their sanity. I tried to get us a table earlier."

"We can talk here," Mark said, dropping his bag.

"Well, don't sit down, for Christ's sake. We'll both be lost at sea. Anyway, you can save all the excuses you've been inventing for another day." Chester was inching his way toward the sofa's arm, and the effort made it impossible for him to talk until he was firmly anchored. "You're off the hook."

"What happened?"

Chester pointed to the red sofa beside his. "Sit down now so I don't have to announce it to the entire campus."

Mark sat as commanded.

"It's the usual story of bargaining and begging. I've been granted a reprieve for one more year on my own. I don't know if I'll have cracked the code of the Housman by next summer—I'm more certain than ever that at least six of those poems are out of proper sequence—but Marjorie has promised not to divorce me if we are living full-time in South Carolina by then."

"So, your office will remain your office till you leave," Mark said. This did register as a relief for Mark, but it also registered as a fair compromise. "That seems right."

Chester grabbed Mark's forearm. "Just because I'm old?" He waited a few seconds to loosen his grip.

"I was thinking more of fair play," Mark said. "And, as you pointed out, it does let me off the hook."

"Fair enough," Chester said. And after Mark helped him out of that sofa, he mystifyingly added, "Just so there's no ill will between us," and excused himself "to find the Gents'," which had been replaced by gender-neutral facilities seven years ago.

4.

Penelope was due at his office at one o'clock. This left Mark fifteen minutes to stare at the final-grade form from the dean, which was more rewarding than staring at Anton's crumpled-up car coat on the floor. Considered together, the abandoned coat and the blank form became a kind of pictograph—cryptic, but imbued with a maudlin significance. If either one was filled out, the other would remain empty.

Mark slipped the form into his bag. The coat was too puffy to stuff into a desk drawer, so he hung it from the hook on his office door, where it immediately looked intolerably poignant. But Penelope knocked, so he grabbed Karen Cole's little chair and wheeled it across the room to hold open the door and hide the effigy of Anton.

Penelope had revised all three Technical Exercises, which Mark read aloud and annotated with just a few questions about motive. The syntax was spot-on, and Penelope enthusiastically endorsed Mark's reservations and suggestions, so the meeting would have taken only ten minutes but for the hurricane that was unleashed each time she dove into her bag to find a sheet of paper or a pen. After an especially big blow, she ducked down and plucked a car key off the floor that she'd reported stolen last semester. In between the storms, she filled Mark in on the progress on her senior thesis, which both she and Nina agreed could never have happened if they hadn't taken the creative-writing course. And had she told Mark how much she loved the course? Nina, too. Nina said it was the best course on campus, and Penelope was telling everyone in her lab to take it.

"Somewhere in here I also have copies of my story if you want them," she said, bent over, her head halfway inside her bag.

"Oh, please, just hand them out in class today," Mark said, hoping to avoid another tempest. "Your workshop is on Wednesday, right?"

"So that's my other question." Penelope dropped her bag and shoveled in the mess she'd made. "On that next Monday after spring break, I might not make it back in time for class."

Not exactly a question, but Mark now understood that the compliments had been a sort of down payment. "Thanks for letting me know," Mark said.

"I can email my comments to Charles and Isaac if I miss their workshops."

"And Julio," Mark said. "Great."

"So it won't count against my grade or anything, my not being there?"

"Well, you won't get credit for not being there, of course."

"No, of course." Penelope was toying with that key, as if she might be able to trade it for some special consideration.

"My family rented a house in Saint John," she said.

"That sounds terrific," Mark said.

"But I won't get, like, points off."

"You won't get anything," Mark said. "Listen, Penelope, I think you're a great member of the workshop, and the stories are getting stronger with every revision. On Monday after break, I won't think less of you. I'll just know you chose not to be in class."

"I could have made up an excuse, a better one." This wasn't a complaint. She seemed to be really thinking about her options.

"You're absolutely right," Mark said. "But I'm not handing out points for honesty, either."

"I don't wish I lied to you," she said as she stood up, "but it's complicated, all this currency business." She slung her bag over her shoulder. "Thanks for your help with those stories. Really."

"You're welcome," Mark said, and as she paused in the doorway, he added, "honestly."

Jane had been hovering for a while, and she was not pleased that Mark hadn't responded to her pacing and sighing in the hall. Now, she had "less than seven minutes and counting," and she needed Mark to spell out the requirements for the rest of the semester "more clearly than you do in class when you allow everyone else to ask irrelevant questions that make it impossible to concentrate." Plus, she wanted to change the date of her workshop, but she instructed him not to think about that until he had cleared up the schedule confusion.

It occurred to him that Jane might be one of the two students the dean had mentioned who had not declared to him their learning challenges or cognitive quirks. "Tell me if I'm speaking too quickly," he said. He explained that her final portfolio had to include one, two, or all three of the Technical Exercises, both original short stories she'd be writing for the rest of the semester, and revisions of all of these had to be shown to the whole class at least once. Mark would respond to as many revisions as Jane produced. "And on Wednesday, I'll assign you one final Technical Exercise that must be in your portfolio, which I will not read or review in advance."

"Or even talk to me about," Jane said, as she wrote. "Go on, go on. I'm all caught up."

"That's it. You have a workshop date for both original stories, and you can bring in copies of revisions to the class whenever you're ready to hear what the others have to say about them."

"That would be approximately never," Jane said. "And I need to change my workshop to the Monday after spring break instead of that Wednesday. Do I have to come up with a reason for that?"

"You just need to be in touch with Charles, Isaac, and Julio and hope one of them is willing to delay his workshop and trade."

"You're saying it's up to me?"

Mark said, "I think I'm saying exactly what it says on the syllabus."

She was already packing up. "I have a midterm later today, so if I'm not as good as usual in class, at least you'll know why."

On her way out, Jane brushed past Rita Jebdi, who was either later than ever for the Romantics or not holding class today. "Did Althea speak to you?"

"I saw her earlier, but we haven't spoken." Mark stood up. "You look elegant today."

"Althea wants you to stop by her office before you leave campus. Maybe this is about our next chair?" Rita spun around. "My sister sent me this crazy tunic thing from Nepal, and I sort of love it. My class is taking a midterm, so I'm celebrating. Also campaigning, to be honest. I put my name in the running for chair."

"You have my vote. You have my endorsement. You have my eternal gratitude."

"Really? I was afraid we might be competing against each other. Oh, my gravy, you have yet another student-in-waiting." As she rippled down the hall, she called out, "Thanks, Mark."

Leo wanted to discuss two sentences in two Technical Exercises, which took about two minutes. He looked disappointed that Mark had nothing more on offer.

"Is there something else you want to talk about, Leo?"

"Not really," he said, but he didn't move.

Mark said, "Midterms?"

Leo said, "None this semester."

Mark said, "Going away for spring break?"

Leo nodded, but he didn't offer up a destination.

This was more dentistry than discussion. Mark steadied his aim and pointed his pliers. "How is the photography project getting on?"

Leo extracted a contact sheet from his notebook. "If you really want to see them, these are the pictures I took of our classroom."

There were twelve little squares, each from a different position around the table. Mark couldn't discern a pattern or a sequence. "They are elegant. The light is especially strange."

"Sort of sad, I think," Leo said. "I ended up liking these better than the color prints." He wasn't offering any other hints.

Mark stood up and handed the sheet to Leo. "Hold them up for me." As he backed away, he saw what Leo had done. "It's your chair—where you usually sit—from twelve different perspectives."

"It's how people see me or don't see me," Leo said. "I think you're the only one who can always see everyone."

That seemed truer than ever soon after Leo left, as Mark stared past the open door into the quiet hallway, mindful of Anton, and his mother, and the dean, who were all trying to figure out how to do their jobs under the worst of circumstances. He pulled the form from his bag a few times, but he didn't fill in any of the blanks. At some point, his Sisyphean paper shuffle was interrupted by Althea Morgan, who sat in the alumni chair and pulled the plastic chair away from the door to use as a footrest.

She was disappointed that Mark would not agree to run the department, largely because she correctly guessed that Rita would lay waste to her impeccable office and military-grade filing system. "I suppose it won't bother anyone when she's half an hour late to departmental meetings," she added.

"It's why I'm voting for her," Mark said. By then, the door had slowly swung shut. He fixed his gaze on Althea.

"At least she's smart," Althea said.

"And good-hearted."

"Loyal," Althea said.

"Stylish," Mark said.

"Honestly, you think she'll be all right as chair?"

Mark said, "Train wreck."

"Yup," Althea said. "Oh, well, you can always lean on Norman Chester, if you can pry him out of that ridiculous chair. He told me he's staying on for another year—with private accommodations, no less."

"I'm surprised the administration relented on the office-sharing," Mark said.

"Not for nothing. They're forcing him to teach a course."

Mark straightened up in his chair. "Housman?"

"No, no. Not a real course. He's doing an Independent Study of some kind. He was in my office for about an hour this morning, forcing me to print out all the forms he'd need, including a final-grade sheet, as he refuses to go online for anything."

Mark was staring at Anton's coat. "Why does he need a final-grade form now?"

Althea shrugged off that question. "It's always hard to tell whether he's sneaky or senile. Take your pick."

"That's one mystery solved," Mark said. He was remembering Chester's odd parting shot in the library—*just so there's no ill will between us.*

"What mystery is that?"

"Norman Chester is not crazy," Mark said.

5.

Althea walked in companionable silence with Mark halfway around the pond, which prevented his taking a detour to dump Norman Chester out of his Morris chair on the way to class. When he got to the classroom, he had only a few minutes before the workshops for Dorothy, Max, and Rashid got underway, which he used to spell out the portfolio requirements one more time. Everyone took notes except Jane, who covered her ears with her hands. He asked Penelope, Virginia, and Leo to pass around copies of their stories, which would be under discussion on Wednesday, and then called out,

"Charles, Isaac, Julio—next time?" Each of them nodded, acknowledging that copies were due on Wednesday for reading over spring break. Dorothy, Willa, Max, and Virginia passed around copies of oft-revised Technical Exercises they were ready to show to their classmates.

Julio said, "Where's Anton?"

"Not here," the Professor said. "Fortunately, the prose in all three of the stories under consideration today is well-made. I'll say more about each one in sequence, but I want to take a few minutes to address the problem of the ending, a problem which inheres in all three of these estimable first drafts."

Leo said, "We haven't talked about endings very much."

The Professor said, "Evidently not often enough."

Max said, "Are you really going to tell everyone what the three of us should have done before the workshops?"

The Professor said, "Do you seriously think that speech from the brother-in-law is the end of the profound story you had going up to that moment?"

Max cocked his head to the side, like a bird responding to an unfamiliar song.

"That speech does seem sort of canned, Max, like you imported it from somewhere else," Dorothy said.

The Professor turned to Dorothy and said, "And why does the friend of the narrator get the last word in your story?"

"It was meant to be ironic," Dorothy said.

The Professor said, "Why?"

Penelope said, "But it is ironic."

"He gets that," Rashid said. "He means why was she aiming for irony? I did the same thing, I think."

"Yes and no," the Professor said. "You did it, Rashid, to avoid having to untangle the very real trauma that bereaved mother has occasioned in her neighborhood and her marriage by doling out those secondhand baked goods. I think Dorothy can't decide whether her narrator's rage about being betrayed was justified or not, so she let the friend at least halfway off the hook with that ironic little joke, which leaves us with no confident sense of the writer's point of view."

Charles said, "This is going well."

"And he said these are good stories," Julio said. "I am so screwed."

"The beginning of your story contains the ending," the Professor said. "That's not a Zen koan, that's advice."

Mark scanned the room. No one had moved. "A pen and paper might be in order," he said.

"The ending has to be a possibility that is present from the start," the Professor said. "We often imagine our characters as actors on a stage while we are writing, but you don't want readers to feel that the story simply stops when you pull the curtain and turn on the house lights. You have to find ways throughout the story to generate a sense of ongoing life, a future beyond the frame of the immediate story. And you have to craft an ending that allows readers to imagine that life for your characters after the last word. And, finally, for now, one additional piece of advice. Do not give your characters the last word. It's your story, not theirs, and though it can work, a character given the last word is too often reductive or—well—"

"Ironic," said Dorothy and Rashid, almost in unison.

"Or just embarrassing," Max said.

"Dorothy wrote a story," the Professor said. He waited until everyone had shuffled their piles of paper. "She titled it 'The Sleeping Porch.' It is given in the past tense in a very intimate third-person voice, limited to Lena. There are two secondary characters. The story is set in the 1940s in a suburb of Oakland, so history bears on the choices made by these young women. I want to frame our analysis with three questions," which he rattled off in quick succession. "Now, where should we begin?"

Mark scanned the room. Eleven of the twelve windowsills were occupied. Leo's camera equipment and Willa's big blue coat and cowboy hat were sharing Anton's chair. It wasn't a happy ending, but it had been a possibility from the start.

6.

On Tuesday, it snowed half-heartedly all day in Ipswich and came to nothing. Mark divided his time between that final-grade form he didn't fill out and the new stories from Leo, Penelope, and Virginia. Paul was on a two-day tour of rural clinics in Bulgaria, so Mark wrote him an exhaustive account of his dilemma with the dean. Hours later, Paul texted back: *A+.* Mark didn't know if this was an endorsement of his principled stand or Paul's suggested final grade for Anton.

On Wednesday morning, Mark woke to a lot of emails and texts from people who'd read the morning newspaper before he had made coffee. Paul's said, *NYTimes! Read all about it!*

After swiping through the rest of his morning mail, Mark texted back, *While the students are sunbathing in the Caribbean, I'll be selecting ties I'll later regret for appearances on MSNBC and FOX.* He saw two new emails with subject lines referencing the op-ed, so he shut off his phone. He sat at the dining room table to write a story to fulfill the limits of the final Technical Exercise of the semester. Although it was not due until the very last class of the semester, Mark knew he would ignore his novel and squander his spring break on the exercise if he didn't get it done this morning. After an hour of sitting that more nearly approximated Zen meditation than creative writing, he closed his laptop, stuck it in his bag with a vow not to leave campus later today until he had a decent draft written, and then took a long shower.

When he got to campus, most of the faculty spaces in the garage were unoccupied, and as he crossed the Common he had to stand aside to make room for waves of joy-blind students rolling their suitcases away from their last classes on their way to the airport. He figured he wouldn't have any visitors for office hours, so he stopped at Althea Morgan's office to let her boast about her plans for spring break in Jamaica, but when she opened her door, he caught a glimpse of Rita Jebdi beside Althea's desk, pawing through a pile of folders. Althea promised to call him before she left town and then gave him the finger before she shut her door.

When he got to the third floor, he saw Julio sitting outside his office, bowed over an open textbook. He didn't say anything. He opened the door, and Julio collected his stuff and sat in the alumni chair. Mark hung his parka over the longer red one on the back of his door, hoping to prevent any questions about Anton's absence.

Julio said, "Have you ever had that dream where you have to take an exam and you suddenly realize you didn't ever go to class?"

"I do know that dream," Mark said as he sat down. "It's unnerving."

"I know." Julio shoved the textbook into his bag and pulled out a stack of paper. "But it's worse if you're me, and you really didn't go to Statistics for like two weeks and you have the midterm tomorrow."

Mark said, "Were you sick?"

"I am now," Julio said, and he handed Mark two revised Technical Exercises.

He had improved both drafts, and after he reviewed Mark's questions and suggestions, he asked Mark to look over a checklist of writing tips he'd translated from his class notes so he could use it from now on. Mark offered a few corrections to the checklist—Julio was still stingy with his commas, and the conventions for punctuating conversations were a revelation to him. Mark assured him that dialogue was especially tricky for second-language speakers. "Isn't it entirely different in Spanish?"

"Probably," Julio said, "but I honestly never paid much attention to it," and then he asked Mark to look at a couple of his essays for other classes. The first was a draft for Comp Lit due before spring break, and Mark underlined a few problematic sentences on the first page and then suggested Julio use his checklist to identify other problems and correct them. Next was a seven-page essay that had already been graded—B+—with a total of six marginal comments from Julio's history professor, the longest of which was *wow! now you're talking.*

Mark underlined several problematic clauses on the first page.

Julio cross-checked them with his chart. "I guess he gives extra credit for comma splices," he said.

"This is the real work, Julio—being better than people expect you to be."

"I'm really trying. You know, in my defense, I didn't start off expecting to have to learn anything in creative writing," Julio said. He didn't sound entirely grateful. "Would you mind if I came back sometimes just to double-check other things I write? Just on the first page, so I know how I'm doing?"

"Bring your checklist."

"And my grade?"

Mark nodded. "In the ascendancy."

Julio didn't say anything.

Mark said, "As in ascending, going up."

"No, no, I get it," Julio said. "Like in my horoscope."

Which, if Mark were being honest, was about as scientific as his grading system.

7.

Mark and the Professor arrived at the classroom at the same moment, and the surprise of seeing all twelve of the chairs at either side of the table occupied, and Max leaning over to point out something on a map to Anton, was displaced by Jane, who announced that the drafts of the stories for the Monday after break had already been distributed.

"I switched with Julio," she explained, "which means that his copies aren't due until the day we get back, and just so you remember, I was already finished writing my story before you told us about endings, and so I'd rather not get a lot of criticism about anything that's not really my fault."

"I'll give you an ending," Max said. "I wrote a long one I won't be using." He had swapped his trademark silky white shirt for an unlikely red-plaid flannel.

Mark said, "Any new revisions?"

Several hands shot up.

"To the right," Mark said. "Please, pass to the right so there's some chance we'll all get one of each."

"My father sent me your article from the *New York Times*." This was Dorothy. "Why didn't you tell us?"

Mark froze up. He did everything he could to keep his own work out of the way in the classroom, but he didn't have a contingency plan today.

Max said, "No series commas, I noticed. What's the world coming to?"

Mark was basically comatose.

The Professor said, "We have first-person stories today from Leo—comma—Penelope—comma—and Virginia—period."

Mark said, "And to make sure we give all three their due, I want to take five minutes now to give you the final Technical Exercise for the semester."

Someone said, "Right back to the beginning."

Jane said, "This is the one you refuse to read until it's too late?"

Willa said, "This is entirely separate from our second short stories, right?"

Mark said, "Yes, and yes."

Charles said, "Is this Technical Exercise Number Four or Five?"

Anton said, "Five."

Isaac said, "Four."

Virginia said, "What if we're only revising one of the first three for our portfolio? Wouldn't this be Number Two?"

The Professor said, "We'll sort out the math after spring break."

Isaac said, "Why do we have to read it out loud at the last class?"

Mark said, "To hear what your readers think about what you've done."

Jane was nodding like mad. "When it's too late to revise."

Rashid said, "Criticism is the highest praise."

Max said, "You live by the word, you die by the word."

The Professor said, "The challenge is to write a satisfying story about a simple situation that lasts for just a few minutes." He paused to give everyone time to find a pen and a blank page.

Dorothy said, "Scenario?"

The Professor said, "The setting is an indoor space outfitted with seating where some event is about to take place—a theater, a chapel, a gymnasium. Before the event begins, all of the seats are occupied but one. Your story opens a few minutes before whatever is about to happen in your imagined space. The central character is a person I will here refer to as X. Next to X is the only empty seat. The story ends just before the event begins—maybe the house lights go down, the first note is sounded on an organ, the stage curtain is raised or parted, or perhaps the narration simply makes it clear that the moment is at hand." He paused until most pens had stopped moving. "Your job is to write the story. Assume your readers know nothing when you begin. Identify as many characters as the story needs, but make X the central character."

Rashid said, "Technical Limits?"

Mark said, "No more than five hundred words." This occasioned a lot of groaning.

Mark said, "Your narrator can use past- or present-tense verbs to tell the story. You must use third-person narration."

Leo said, "Limited or omniscient?"

"Your choice," Mark said. "But I want to urge you to infuse the narration with authority about the setting, the situation, and the emotional or psychological stakes. Look for opportunities to let your narrator make a few big, bold statements. Take some risks with your authorial power."

Leo said, "And every other word must begin with the letter *X*."

Isaac said, "Do we have to name her X?"

"Wild guess." This was Anton. "We give her a normal name."

Charles said, "How do you know it's a *she* and not a *he* or a *they*?"

Mark said, "We won't know until the stories are written."

Penelope asked if the seat next to X had to remain empty.

"No," Mark said, "and you assign gender as you see fit. But the lived time of the story is no more than five minutes." He let that sink in.

Julio asked how many people were in the audience.

"That's up to you. But it will help to let readers know how many people are in attendance," Mark said. "There really are no other limits, but there is one reminder: The principal arena for the action is the space you invent, and that empty chair will be significant to readers as soon as you alert them to its existence. Something ought to happen there."

Max said, "Action."

Rashid said, "Is."

Dorothy said, "Not going to be easy if almost all of our characters are in their seats from the start."

Mark sat and let the workshops begin. All twelve windowsills were occupied. He opened his notebook and didn't close it until Virginia had collected the last of her comments from the other writers, and Isaac had yelled, "Spring is here, baby," and everything he had piled up for return had been taken, and only Anton remained, standing beside him.

"Did you by any chance get my email?"

Mark said, "I haven't looked at my phone for a while."

Anton said, "I should've come by before class to warn you I want to talk to you." He walked to the door and turned from the threshold. "I have to drop off a form in College Hall before they close. Will you be in your office in, say, fifteen minutes?"

"I will," Mark said.

Mark found his phone and waited in the classroom for it to come to life. He had twenty-one new emails, including three from the dean of students. The first was a request for Mark to call him before noon. The second was a request for Mark to call him before his class met. The third began with a request for Mark to let him know he had received what followed, which was followed by an apology—"I am sorry not to do this in person, which was my intention"—which turned out to be the preface to a longer apology.

Braxton was sorry for having involved Mark in the confusion. He had spoken again to Anton's mother. She didn't know if Anton would or would not be in class today. She had shown all of the paperwork to Anton's stepfather, and he ("correctly," Braxton inserted) understood for the first time that if Anton received a final grade and a degree, the college would not ("COULD NOT" Braxton inserted) allow him to withdraw officially and refund the 50 percent of tuition, room and board, and fees for the semester. Braxton had written to Anton to determine whether he intended to withdraw or not, but he had not yet had a response. He did not mention how this might affect the fate of Norman Chester's Morris chair, but he did paste in an email exchange with the stepfather from February, in which the dean had confirmed that the nongovernmental loan program the family had used to finance Anton's fifth year did not carry a death rider and that the only relief the college could offer would require Anton to withdraw, in which case the debt would be prorated and decreased considerably.

The exchange ended with a note Braxton had written when he'd forwarded all of this to the vice president for Academic Affairs: "The parents seemed to think the student could withdraw from the college and still graduate!"

Of course, this was effectively the scheme Braxton had proposed to Mark—minus the official withdrawal, plus $15,000 or $20,000 for the second half of the semester. Mark wrote an email highlighting this hypocrisy, reread it, and then revised it, and then revised it once again so it finally read: *Got it.* He packed up and headed to Hum Hall.

Anton was seated on an overstuffed knapsack topped off with a sleeping bag when Mark unlocked his office. He left his bag in the hall and slipped into the alumni chair. As Mark sat at his desk, the door swung shut.

Anton turned briefly and said, "Thanks for hanging that up."

Mark said, "You do know you are not leaving this building without it, right?"

Anton nodded. "If you know anyone who wants a shiny red car coat, tell them to check out eBay this weekend. I really revised the tag sale story—it's in your pile—but right now I need to talk to you about something else." He unwound the scarf from his neck. "I wore it every day," he said, holding it aloft for a moment before letting it droop over the arm of the chair. Apparently, he'd also worn the same black turtleneck sweater and lined jeans for the last week, and not eaten enough. He looked frail, though his skin was a normal color again. "It's supposed to be pretty warm for the next couple of days," he said, "even at night, I heard." He tugged at the neck of his sweater. "Did you hear that?"

Mark nodded.

Anton said, "That's what I heard, too. How warm is it supposed to be? At night, I mean."

"I doubt it will be tropical," Mark said.

Anton said, "But warm enough."

"I honestly haven't been paying close attention," Mark said, hoping the weather discussion would soon give way to whatever they weren't talking about yet.

Anton didn't say anything for a while.

Mark said, "And?"

Anton said, "Well, my first full-length story—the one due after spring break about the sick kid in the cross-country race? I scrapped it."

Mark said, "For good?"

"Last weekend, I was reading the stories Max and Rashid and Dorothy wrote—I know you thought they had problems, but they're all way better than what I'd written so far. I mean, really in another league, so I got thinking about that optional Technical Exercise you gave us with the mother who's a waitress with the little kid who might or might not be dead when she gets home from work after leaving him home alone all day."

So, Anton was back. This story had another chapter.

Anton said, "You know, the one with the dog nobody wants outside the diner?"

Mark nodded. "You could decide to make the other story—the one about the two runners—your second story."

"The one with the sick guy, you mean?"

Mark nodded.

Anton nodded, but he said, "I doubt it. Max has more ideas about how to write it than I do."

Anton had seen his limits. If he didn't yet sound as if he loved them, he was regarding them, responding to them. Mark said, "And you have time to get a full draft done of the long Technical Exercise?"

"The thing is, I can't get that kid out of my mind for some reason, and he doesn't have to be dead or kidnapped or anything at the end, right? I mean, that waitress might not even be a bad mother if you can make people see why she left that kid alone, right?"

"Right and right," Mark said. "It's your story," and maybe it had been Anton's story before the stepfather turned up.

"I have all next week to work on it," Anton said. "I'm staying on campus—that's the form I had to drop off at College Hall. They don't charge you extra, but you have to let them know if you're planning to be here so there's enough food and dining-hall workers. Max is staying, too. He's directing some choir or opera chorus, and rehearsals start next week. I'm supposed to meet him soon—like ten minutes ago, I think."

Mark nodded.

Anton didn't say anything.

Mark said, "And?"

Anton said, "Oh, you know me, Mark—and, and, and." He stood up, but instead of turning to the door, he walked past Mark and leaned into the windowsill, his shoulders heaving. He turned halfway toward Mark and said, "I'm not crying again. I'm just thinking."

Mark said, "Okay," though he really didn't understand how Anton ever managed to think without crying.

After a long while, the heavy breathing subsided, and Anton straightened up and sat on the little white desk.

Mark said, "We're going to have to use words."

Anton smiled. "You and your words." He looked down accusingly at the desk. It wasn't as comfortable a landing pad as he'd expected. He hopped down and returned to the alumni chair. "Let's face it, you'd have to be an idiot to believe what they say, right?"

"Try me," Mark said.

"I knew you'd want to know, so I've been trying to think about how to say it so you wouldn't think—well, so you could see how I'm trying to look at it."

Mark said, "And, and, and."

"I know, I know," Anton said, smiling. "So on Monday, it ended up being not so bad. I'm not switching drugs after all, so that's better than we thought last time, right?"

Mark nodded.

"All the memory stuff we were worried about when I talked to you a few weeks ago? That's mostly not happening, some days not at all. My numbers—you know how they can measure your blood cells and everything? The numbers were flying all over the place last week, but the scans were not bad." He glanced back at his coat and said, "I mean, they were sort of clear for some reason. Not clean, but pretty clear, if you know what I mean."

Mark said, "Much less bad stuff, much more good stuff."

"Exactly," Anton said.

"Got it, "Mark said.

"So, now I guess we'll see," Anton said.

Mark said, "Exactly."

Anton wound the scarf around his neck. "Do you remember that tepee? The one in that other Forbes room where you came and found me on the first day of class?"

Mark nodded. "I was lost, too," he said.

Anton evidently doubted that, but he didn't argue the point. He said, "Was it real?"

"I don't know if it was made out of buffalo hide, or maybe canvas, but I remember being told it was real—a ceremonial item, maybe a gift to the college?" Mark had no idea where this was going.

"But you do think it's real, and weatherproof, probably," Anton said.

Mark didn't say anything.

A knock at the door startled them both, and they stood up in unison.

Someone sang out, "Oh, Professor?" Soon, in a deeper voice, he sang, "Oh, oh, oh, dear Professor!"

Anton opened the door.

Max was bent forward a bit under the weight of a knapsack and sleeping bag strapped over his red-plaid flannel shirt, the pocket of which was now festooned with a corncob pipe. "It's almost six o'clock, Anton. I'm sorry to intrude, Mark, but in case you haven't heard, they dropped the bomb, the mushroom cloud is expanding, and the campus has been evacuated."

Anton stepped around the open door and snagged his coat. "I'm ready. We're done." He turned to Mark. "We are done, right?"

"So done," Mark said. Max hadn't been there long, but it was just long enough for Mark to assemble all of the suggestive material that had been accumulating since he noticed them poring over that map in the classroom. He could now see where this story was going to end.

Max said, "What are you doing over the break, Mark?"

"Let me tell you what I am not doing," Mark said, tipping back in his chair. "I am not fielding a phone call from the campus police about two idiots sleeping in a stolen tepee in Breakheart Reservation with a case of beer or a pipe full of something and a campfire that has spread to campus and burned down our classroom."

Anton twisted his face up into a confused expression, and when even he could tell that wasn't working, he tried again with a conspiratorial shrug.

Mark shook his head.

Max said, "Anton was a Boy Scout."

As if to prove the point, Anton hoisted his knapsack onto his back and stood at attention beside Max.

Mark pulled his phone out of his bag.

Anton said, "What are you doing?"

Mark said, "Putting the dean of students and the vice president for Academic Affairs on speed dial."

"You can trust us," Anton said.

"It's an artifact, not a pup tent," Mark said.

"We're all packed," Max said, and then he tilted sideways against the threshold, as if he might be about to faint under the weight of his gear.

Mark slammed his phone on the desk. "Don't your rooms have balconies? Sleep out there." He didn't itemize exactly what was at stake for second-semester seniors—one of them still enrolled by the skin of his teeth. "Rent an RV and find a campground that actually allows overnight camping." He didn't remind Max that his parents would end up footing the bill for the full semester if he was tossed out of the college without a degree. He didn't regale Anton with the practical limits of his severely compromised immune system. He did think about hoisting Max up by his man bun so he could bang their heads together.

Anton said, "Everyone else is going to Tahiti."

Max said, "That RV is not a half-bad idea."

Anton said, "Can we afford that?"

Max nodded. "Probably cheaper than bail."

"Go away," Mark said. "Please, go away."

"Okay, okay," Anton said.

"We will be back," Max said.

"I know, I know," Mark said wearily. He didn't say so—at that moment, he didn't know it—but when they turned up again, he would be happy to see them. He watched the office door swing shut, and then he extracted his laptop from his bag. While he waited for it to light up, he felt the weight of having invented a new story to fulfill the limits of this final Technical Exercise every semester for ten years as if it were a knapsack on his back.

How big would a room have to be to hold all of the Creative Writing students he had taught at Hellman? For lack of a better idea, he attempted to do the math.

For nine years, he had taught two sections of twelve students in the fall and spring. Add to that this tenth year with a reduced course load for NEPCAJE meetings. Double all of that to accommodate the twelve writers who turned up and took their places at the table at some point during the semester, displacing the students to the windowsills. And then he had to make space for himself and the Professor. He lost count while debating whether they should account for two seats in his vast classroom, or if he should furnish them with additional chairs to represent every iteration of the course.

Whose story was this? He could make Max the protagonist, which would make the empty chair Anton's. If it was Rashid's story, and Rashid was waiting for Charles to arrive and take a seat, the drama could turn on whether Charles appeared or whether Charles appeared as a *he*, *she*, or *they*. He imagined his way around the room, one potential protagonist at a time.

Mark still hadn't written a word. He spent hours in his office, as he had spent ten years in the classroom, cultivating each of those twelve possibilities. Whoever's story this was, Mark knew that the central character would not come from among those twelve writers at the table, who would soon find themselves at other tables acting as lawyers and singers and stepfathers and doctors, inhabiting roles that had once seemed unimaginable or unnerving or simply beyond their limits. The central character would not come from among the twelve students seated on the windowsills, watching and marveling at and worrying about what they were doing at the table. Those twelve static figures in the windows knew their limits—we all do—but they did not yet love them. In their lives, their limits had been humiliating or frustrating, frightening or depressing, defining what they could not do, encompassing all they would never be.

Mark knew neither he nor the Professor could be the central character. A genuine character would emerge from that indeterminate space between the chairs at the table and the windowsills, the breach between Mark and the Professor. This was not a place where people lived beyond or without limits. It was not even a habitable space. It was a moment. It was an opportunity available in the classroom to measure the distance between our intentions and our achievements, the chance to learn to love the lifelong work of mending that gap.

TECHNICAL EXERCISE 5: LAST CLASS

The rain had come suddenly and hard while the students were shouting their thanks and goodbyes, bemoaning Mark's announcement that he would not be on campus for commencement, making promises to be in touch, and angling for leniency on their final grades, so it was not until they were all gone that Mark thought to close the wide-open windows. He pulled the last one down and watched the chaotic end of the semester on the Common, the students rushing around the pond, heads disappearing beneath hoods and umbrellas, their familiar shapes melting into the other bodies streaming across campus to freedom.

Mark was leaving tomorrow morning for a month in Rome, and as he had been sleeping at Paul's place for the last several weeks to mitigate the distance between them, he had not been to Ipswich to locate a suitcase, never mind pack. Presently, though, he was waiting for the Professor to turn up. He and Mark always came together after the last class to assign a provisional grade for each student. It was reliably contentious, and often so unpleasant that they didn't communicate for a week afterward, time enough for Mark to read the final portfolios—which the Professor considered an exercise in redundancy. As he liked to say, he didn't believe in miracles. The

Professor's neglect of this duty gave Mark leverage, which he used to raise everybody's official final grade.

He had an endless supply of As. Where else was he going to spend them?

As the rain obliterated his view of the campus, Mark retreated to his chair at the head of the room, set his bag on the Professor's chair, as he did every day of every semester, and reached in for his notebook and a pen. The crowd streamed in, students from across the years arriving in waves, hoisting each other up onto each windowsill, a dozen at a time, and then the later waves took to the chairs until every seat was shared by four, with four more perched on every arm, and still dozens more were rolling in, shoving their way into the open space below and then on top of the table, closing up even that gap between the Professor's chair and his.

Mark couldn't imagine how the classroom could accommodate anyone else. He couldn't even see the door. And yet, there would be another wave of students arriving in September, and more again rolling in next spring. Where was the Professor? He saw hundreds of faces turned to him, hopeful and anxious wide-eyed gazes fixed on the front of the room, and he couldn't get a clear view of anything else, not even the chair next to his.

There was no Professor beside Mark. Every student could plainly see that there had never been a Professor besides Mark. Of course, the man they saw cared as much about their commas and conjunctions as he did about a catastrophic illness or their capacity for kindness. That was Creative Writing.

(499 words)

END

Acknowledgments

This book exists thanks to the faith and forbearance of my editor, Jack Shoemaker, and my agent, Gail Hochman; the great work done by Megan Fishmann, Jordan Koluch, Jennifer Alton, Yuki Tominaga, Denise Silva, and everyone at Counterpoint; the intelligence and indulgence of Mary Ann Matthews and Michelle Blake; the sustaining enthusiasm of Alexandra Zapruder, Henry Bolter, Marcia Folsom, Diana Shaw Clark, and Monica Klien; and, as ever, first and foremost, Peter Bryant. And the dumplings at Mary Chung.

© Frank Monkiewicz

MICHAEL DOWNING is the author of nine books, including the national bestseller *Perfect Agreement*; *Breakfast with Scot*, which was adapted as a feature film; *Shoes Outside the Door: Desire, Devotion, and Excess at San Francisco Zen Center*; and *Spring Forward: The Annual Madness of Daylight Saving Time*. A frequent commentator in the national media on Congress and the clocks, he teaches creative writing at Tufts University. Find more at michaeldowningbooks.com.